Copyright 2012

Laurence E Dahners

Kindle Edition

ISBN: 978-1477671504
ASIN: B007418CL2

Smarter

An Ell Donsaii story #2

Laurence E Dahners

Author's Note

Though this book can "stand alone" it'll be much easier to understand if read as part of the series beginning with "Quicker (an Ell Donsaii story)." I've minimized the repetition of explanations that would be redundant to the first book in order to provide a better reading

Other Books and Series
by Laurence E Dahners

Series
The Hyllis Family series
The Vaz series
The Bonesetter series
The Blindspot series
The Proton Field series

Single books (not in series)
The Transmuter's Daughter
Six Bits
Shy Kids Can Make Friends Too

For the most up to date information go to
Laury.Dahners.com/stories.html

Table of Contents

Preprologue

Ell's father, Allan Donsaii, was an unusually gifted quarterback. Startlingly strong, and a phenomenally accurate passer, during his college career he finished two full seasons without any interceptions and two games with 100 percent completions. Unfortunately, he wasn't big enough to be drafted by the pros.

Extraordinarily quick, Ell's mother, Kristen Taylor captained her college soccer team and rarely played a game without a steal.

Allan and Kristen dated more and more seriously through college, marrying at the end of their senior year. Their friends teased them that they'd only married so they could start their own sports dynasty.

Their daughter Ell has Kristen's quickness, magnified by Allan's surprising strength and highly accurate coordination.

She *also* has a new mutation that affects the myelin sheaths of her nerves. This mutation produces nerve transmission speeds nearly double those of normal neurons. With faster nerve impulse transmission, she has *far* quicker reflexes. Yet her new type of myelin sheath is also thinner, allowing more axons, and therefore more neurons, to be packed into the same sized skull. These two factors result in a brain with more neurons, though it isn't larger, *and* a faster processing speed, akin to a computer with a smaller, faster CPU architecture.

Most importantly, under the influence of adrenalin in a fight or flight situation, her nerves transmit even more rapidly than their normally remarkable speed.

Much more rapidly...

Prologue

Most of a year had passed since that fateful second day at the Dallas Olympics. President Teller had agreed to give the commencement speech at the Air Force Academy. After Teller had spoken and the cadets had received their diplomas in the traditional fashion, the Commandant of the Academy said, "Now I have the privilege of turning the podium back over to the President of the United States. Mr. President?"

The President stepped back to the podium. "I am sure that most of you will not be surprised to find that my next words have something to do with a most unusual cadet that you have amongst your ranks." He looked out over the assembled cadets, "Ms. Donsaii, I believe 'front and center' is the usual command at such times?"

Everyone waited patiently as Ell got up from her seat out in the audience and marched her way to the front. She approached the podium and to her surprise she suddenly recognized Chief Bowers and Jamal Assad seated among the dignitaries on the stage! Despite a mental hiccough she turned smoothly and saluted the President.

He returned the salute, then turned back to the audience and cameras. "I'm sure you're all aware that, before her participation was interrupted by a terrorist attack, Ms. Donsaii won *four* back to back individual gold medals in Gymnastics at the Olympic Games last summer." He paused for thunderous applause to surge up and gradually die out.

"Unless you were living under a rock, I'm sure you are also aware of the role she played in frustrating the plans of those terrorists. After escaping to warn us, she purposefully allowed herself to be recaptured by the terrorists and then single handedly killed or disabled eight extremists, thus saving the lives of twenty-eight Team USA athletes including one of your fellow cadets and Olympic Silver Medalist, Mr. Phillip Zabrisk." The President paused again for tumultuous cheering to rise up and then gradually subside.

"Today I am proud to announce that, in the name of the Congress of the United States, I am awarding Ms. Donsaii the Medal of Honor 'for conspicuous gallantry and intrepidity at the risk of her life, above and beyond the call of duty, while engaged in action against an enemy of the United States.'" He picked up a case from the podium, opened it and pulled out a ribbon with the medal on it. He held it up to the crowd for a moment, then turned to put it around Ell's neck. Turning back to the microphone he said. "I believe the tradition is that everyone, regardless of rank or status, is encouraged to salute Medal of Honor winners. I wish to be first to do so." He made a creditable left face and rendered Ell a sharp military salute.

Out in the audience Phil elbowed Jason, "Actually, I was the first," he whispered.

The President turned back to the microphone, "Company... ten hut!" With a crash the military personnel on the stage and in the audience stood and came to attention. He turned again to Ell and said, "Present arms," and he, as well as all the military personnel present rendered their sharpest salutes. "At ease, and please be seated.

"Now I suppose you might think that we have rendered Ms. Donsaii sufficient honors for one day. However, there are a few things that you probably *aren't* aware of. Ms. Donsaii is not only a physical phenom, able to perform athletically at a level no one had really dreamed possible, but she is undeniably a genius as well. By now most of you are aware that the Academy's rules were bent to allow her to enter at the unheard of age of fifteen. *Some* of you may be aware that when she entered, she essentially tested out of most of the first two years of the academic curriculum here at the Academy. A very few of you are aware, though many of you will be unsurprised to learn, that she has completed the remainder of the academic coursework requirements for graduation in the two years that she has been here. The girl is still under the age of eighteen!

"Furthermore, I am able to announce that today the prestigious scientific journal Nature is publishing a paper that she submitted. A paper entitled 'A Possible Mechanism for Quantum Entanglement through an Unperceived Dimension.' I am assured by those who understand this science, that this paper will stir up the world of physics like very few papers since the publications of Albert Einstein more than a century ago."

The complete stunned silence of the audience was palpable. The President grinned and reached into the podium again. "Thus it is my distinct, if unusual, privilege to award one more graduation diploma today, two years earlier than expected, to Ms. Ell Donsaii. And to inform her that she has offers from MIT, Cal Tech and numerous other schools to enter their graduate programs in physics. I also inform her that her country believes it's in the best interest of these United States that she attend such a graduate school prior to serving her time on active duty." He turned to Ell and handed her the diploma, then saluted her once again, holding it while she returned the salute. They both held their salutes until he whispered, "I'm holding this salute until you drop yours first." He winked. She dropped her salute and the stadium erupted.

Smarter

Chapter One

Ell had mixed feelings as she entered the out-processing office at the Academy. She felt excited about getting on with her life, especially with grad school. She hoped to join a good experimental physics team that could provide her with the tools to investigate some of her quantum theories. Yet she felt sad to be leaving behind many of her cadet classmates, all of whom had another two years to go.

Not unexpectedly, when she arrived at the office she found herself in line with a long wait. It was frustrating that this couldn't be handled over the net, but in the military, formal events like comings and goings still required the signing of actual papers with an obligatory period of heel cooling. As she looked around the waiting room she recognized that a number of other 3rd class cadets were also waiting which puzzled her. Then she realized that they were leaving the academy, taking advantage of the opportunity to quit without owing the active duty commitment that accrued as soon as you started your junior year.

Ell had just begun to wonder how much active duty commitment she would owe when a clerk called her name. When Ell sat down the clerk glanced up at her 3rd class shoulder boards and asked, "You're seeking early departure?"

Ell said, "Well kind of. I graduated yesterday."

The Airman took another startled look at her shoulder boards. "But you're a 3rd class cadet!"

"Yes. But I completed the requirements for graduation so they gave me a diploma yesterday at the graduation ceremony."

Now the clerk glanced at her nametag, "Oh! You're Donsaii! I heard about that." He looked up at her face for the first time, "I'm sorry, I should have recognized you from the Olympics. It's just that the 3rd class uniform threw me off. Let me have my AI pull up your file." He stared at his monitor for a moment. "Ah, OK. Here, I'm sending it to you. You're being assigned to detached duty for grad school. In addition to your five year commitment for the Academy you'll accrue three more years of commitment for each year of grad school. I'm printing out the document for your signature now."

Ell sat up straighter and scanned the document on her e-slate. "Don't waste paper printing that. I won't sign it. There must be other options?"

The clerk frowned as he stared at his monitor and mumbled to his AI. "Sorry Ms. Donsaii. This is the only option available in your file."

"Well that just doesn't make sense. In the first place I don't think I should owe a full five year commitment for two years at the Academy and I'm not certainly not signing up for three years of additional commitment for each year of grad school! If I did four years of grad school I'd owe seventeen years! You were right with the first question you asked me. I'll just sign up for early departure without a commitment!"

"You can't do that! You've already graduated. You owe five years."

"My original enlistment said I'd only owe a commitment when I started my third year at the Academy. I haven't begun my third year. The Academy can't go back on that."

The clerk's eyes widened and he had his AI pull up another document, presumably the original enlistment forms. After studying it for a moment he mumbled, "Let me get the Lieutenant." He got up from his chair and beat a retreat to the back office.

After a few moments he reappeared and motioned Ell into a back hallway.

Ell entered the office and came to attention. The overweight, balding lieutenant behind the desk waved to the lone chair and Ell sat down across from him. "The airman says you're trying to wiggle out of your commitment?"

Ell sighed internally. She hated confrontations like this and in the past might have just backed down, "No sir. I have two issues. First I don't think I should owe five years commitment for two years of education here at the Academy and, second, I don't want to accrue three years commitment for each year of grad school."

The lieutenant's eyebrows rose. "You've graduated. How many years commitment do other graduates owe?"

"They owe five years sir. But they spend four years at the Academy. I do feel it would be reasonable for me to owe a two and a half year active duty commitment."

"You're that *special*, eh?"

Ell winced, "No sir. But the Air Force only made half its usual investment in my education, I don't think it is unreasonable that it get only half the active duty commitment in return."

"Well I, for one, am tired of you being treated like you're better than everyone else Donsaii. You'll owe five years or you aren't getting that diploma. And, if the Air Force is going to pay for your grad school you'll owe three for one on that."

"Begging your pardon sir, but I already have the diploma and I don't want the Air Force to pay for grad school. You're welcome to simply discharge me per my original enlistment if you like."

"Not gonna happen. You aren't getting everything your way on this one Cadet. You'd just as well sign on the dotted line."

This time Ell sighed audibly, "Sir, do you want me to take this up the chain of command?"

"Are you threatening me Cadet?"

"No Sir. Simply exercising my right to take an issue up the chain sir."

"You want to talk to Major Linz?!"

Ell shrugged, "Yes Sir."

The lieutenant got up and stalked out of his office without another word.

After a few minutes Ell turned back to her slate and began running more correlations between known experimental data and the math she'd invented. The math coordinated her proposed extra dimension and quantum behavior.

She was so focused that she was startled when the office door slammed back open and the Lieutenant stalked back in and sat down. "Apparently, Ms. Donsaii, it would be a 'PR debacle' if *you* didn't get your way." The lieutenant's words were clipped but precise. "Would this document meet your satisfaction?"

A window popped open on Ell's e-slate, she expanded it and read the document which released her from active duty effectively now, and would have her resume active duty for two and a half years once she left grad school. Essentially it was the same as if she were discharged, but with a commitment to reenlist and, of course she'd be on reserve status and could be called back up at the nation's need. The Air Force would not support her financially during grad school. She looked up and said, "Yes Sir. This is fine. If you'll print it, I'll sign it."

Icily the Lieutenant said, "You probably should read the whole thing to be sure I didn't slip any clauses in there that you don't like."

Ell's frosty green eyes met his and, realizing that he didn't think she'd had time to read it in the past 60 seconds, she said, "Sir, I did read it. There is an inconsequential substitution of the homonym 'their' for 'there" in the third paragraph but I don't think it needs to be edited. The meaning is clear as written. Thank you."

***

Ell sighed as she walked out the concourse at the ILM airport in Wilmington. She'd spent much of the flight home from Colorado fending off the eager attentions of the two men seated next to her on the flight. They hadn't recognized her as Ell Donsaii, just found her attractive. On one hand it was nice that they thought she was cute, but on the other hand their constant attempts to start conversations kept her from working on her quantum models. And the big one'd had bad breath. She picked her duffle up off the baggage belt and threw the strap over her shoulder. She turned toward the door but then heard her name, "Ms. Donsaii? Oops, I mean Lieutenant Donsaii?" Ell turned to see a mother with two daughters aged somewhere between seven and eleven hurrying toward her.

"Please? Could I get a picture with my daughters?"

Ell smiled and nodded graciously. It had become somewhat irritating to be recognized and stopped so frequently whenever she left the Academy grounds, but she always thought of Michael Fentis' rude refusal to give her an autograph at the Olympics. She'd resolved to be polite every time it happened. Unfortunately, while the one picture was being taken, other people recognized her. They actually formed a line for pictures and autographs. Allan, El's AI (Artificial Intelligence assistant), whispered through her earpiece, "Your mother's now waiting outside."

She turned to the people in the line and said, "My Mom's waiting outside so I can take one more group picture with the rest of you, but then I've got to run." The group accepted the compromise and soon Ell was glancing up at the HUD (Heads Up Display) screens on her AI's headband as it projected an arrow to direct her out to where Kristen's old Nissan sat at the curb. She tossed her duffle in the backseat and jumped in. As the car pulled itself out into traffic Ell leaned over to give her mom a hug. Kristen instructed the car's AI to take them home to Morehead City and they excitedly started catching up on each other's lives.

"...so I owe them two and a half years active duty after I finish grad school."

"How are you going to pay for grad school though?"

"Well, grad students usually get a stipend of some sort for teaching or doing research, plus I'm hoping to get a scholarship from one of the Universities." She shrugged, "I've actually saved quite a bit of my Cadet salary because pretty much everything was paid for at the Academy. I've been pinching the pennies as hard as I can." She shrugged, "I can take out loans if I have to. If

I just *can't* make ends meet, I'll have to go back on active duty. That'll bring me a full officer's salary while I'm in school, but then I'll owe a bigger military time commitment when I'm done."

"I can help a little bit, but you know I don't have a lot of extra cash or I'd be driving a better car than this old junker."

"No problem, Mom." Ell thought it sad. As an attorney Kristen's husband Jake seemed to be fairly well off, but he'd insisted on a prenuptial agreement keeping their finances separate. He pretty much left his wife to get along however she could on her low teacher's and waitressing salaries. Ell wouldn't be surprised if he was charging Kristen rent to live in the house they shared. "Right now I'm more worried about financing some trips to various grad schools for the application process. The places I want to go to probably won't take me without at least an interview."

"Ouch! That could be kind of expensive, maybe I could pay for one of those trips for your birthday?"

"That'd be nice, thanks!"

"Hey, you remember Mr. Mandal, your old guidance counselor?"

"Sure, he helped a lot when I was trying to figure out college."

"Well he's the principal now and asked me if you'd be willing to give the commencement address for the high school graduation?"

"Accch! I'm still a year younger than a lot of the graduates! *They* aren't going to want to hear *me* talk!"

"Believe me, *no one* thinks about your age. You're *much* too famous for anyone to worry about whether you're 'old enough.' He said it'd mean a lot to the school. You're by far their best known graduate."

"I didn't even graduate! I left after my junior year. Besides, isn't graduation in just a couple more days?"

"Saturday. They have another speaker who's agreed to step aside if you're willing."

Ell moaned, "What would I talk about?"

"Tell them about gymnastics and winning the gold medals, that's what they're most interested in."

"But you and I know I'm a freak. I can't just tell them that gymnastics is easy for me."

"Talk to them about physics then."

"They'll die of boredom." Ell threw her head back on the headrest with a little whimper. "Let me think about it for a moment."

"And…"

"And what? You're not going to spring *another* speech on me are you?"

"No. But Jake… Well, I know you and Jake have never gotten along. But he got to be *such* a big fan of yours when you were in the Olympics. And now he's just dying to do something to make it up to you for how he behaved in the past. He's been working hard on something for you all this last week. I don't know what it is, but I hope you'll give him a chance with it?"

"Oh Mom. I don't know. Just hearing his name brings back a picture of that condescending sneer …"

"Please… for me?"

"Arrgh! Okay, I guess you love him and he *is* my step-dad. I'll cut him some slack. Not much though. I just can't picture him giving up his old ways."

"Try to be nice. He might even help finance those interview trips you're worried about."

"Well, actually that *would* be nice."

Smarter

***

Ell's heart started pounding while Mr. Mandal was giving her a glowing introduction. To her dismay he focused on her gymnastic gold medals and her subsequent role in stopping the terrorist plot to derail the Olympics. Ell had hoped that as an educator he'd concentrate on her academic achievements and at least mention her physics paper, especially since that was what she intended to talk about. She stood and, trembling like a leaf inside, slowly walked to the podium. Staring out over the gymnasium full of people she reflected wonderingly to herself that neither competing in the Olympics nor facing terrorists had made her this tremulous. There was just something about public speaking, especially to a group of her peers. She grimaced; they were going to *hate* her topic.

Her fear went unrecognized by the audience who only saw an attractive, slender, strawberry-blond young woman in a black pantsuit get up from her seat and walk, apparently confidently, across the stage to the podium.

She stood silently at the microphone several long moments, wondering if she actually had the courage to give this talk. People shifted in their seats. Finally, she cleared her throat, "I suspect… that you want to hear about winning Olympic gymnastics medals." she said weakly, then cleared her throat again and with more strength said, "Or that you want to hear about what it was like to be in that room with the terrorists.

"OK…

"The first was exhilarating and the second was terrifying…"

Ell paused. At first scattered chuckles, then a full

throated laugh swept the audience. "Now that that's out of the way, let me tell you about something *much* more interesting. At least to me.

"Young's double slit experiment is one of the most elegant and exciting phenomena in all of physics. It's something that *I* lie awake thinking about. I think you should all be puzzled by it too, so I'm going to briefly explain it to you.

"If you send light, say a laser beam, at a narrow slit you'll find that the beam spreads out on the other side of the slit, just like the waves in water do when they come through a narrow opening in a breakwater." Ell felt proud that she'd recognized such an analogy would be readily understood by the people in this coastal town. "If you send that beam so it hits two neighboring slits it will spread out from each slit and create an 'interference' pattern where the waves double up in some areas and block each other out in others. So light must consist of waves right? Well yes light does act like a wave. However, light *also* acts like a particle. You can slow down your light emitting device until it's only emitting one of these particles at a time. These are known as quanta or photons. Then the photons show up at the detector as a single spot, kind of like a bullet hitting a target, and just like a particle would, they leave a mark at that one spot. You can send those particles through the two slits, one at a time, and see each one appear at the detector on the other side of the slits, one at a time, each arriving as a single little spot on that detector. *Just like a particle should arrive.* That's not very wavelike! But, and here's the craziness, after thousands of your photon particles have gone through the two slits, one at a time, you'll find that they've arrived at the target, distributed in that *same* wave interference pattern I told you about before! It's as if the particles act like waves even when they're traveling all by themselves, one at a time! It's *freaking* bizarre, but it's true.

"This phenomenon has given physicists headaches for decades and has led to weird terms like 'wavicles' to try to describe this tendency to act like both a wave and a particle at the same time. So I present this to you as a challenge. Figure this out! Or at least ponder it.

"Now, you probably thought I'd give a long winded speech or try to inspire you with stories of how hard I worked to earn those gold medals in gymnastics. Instead I'm telling you what I *want* to do. I want to figure this 'wavicle' thing out.

"The way I see it, there are two possibilities. First, light is neither a wave, nor a particle, *nor* a wavicle, but instead something completely different from any of those familiar things. If so, we need to come up with a different descriptive model than either a particle or a wave for what light really is. Or, my current pet theory, which is that light's made of single photon particles that can actually spread out like a bunch of particles. In other words, each particle can spread out like a 'wave' of particles and all these spread out 'subphotons' are actually connected to one another through a 5th dimension that we can't see, feel, or touch. Then when the photon arrives at its destination, having traveled like a wave of subphotons, it coalesces through that 5th dimension to become a single complete photon at the one single point where we detect it at our receptor apparatus.

"I'm particularly excited to have invented a math that seems to fit known experimental data correctly for such subphotons and a 5th dimension. At least so far it has. I could be proven wrong at any moment! I want to go to grad school to work on experiments suggested by that math. I'm dying to see if my math continues to agree with even newer experimental results.

"But, it's important that you realize it's *very* likely I'll turn out to be wrong. And so there's plenty of room for millions of bright minds like yours to contemplate other ways that light could travel, neither as a wave, nor as a particle and yet behave like it does in the double slit experiment.

"Or, if you don't want to work on that, there are thousands of other problems out there, from physics to fisheries, from photons to farms, *all* needing solutions. So I urge you to go forth and seek, not just work, but answers to problems of all types!

"Finally, I know that one, or maybe two of you, are disappointed to have heard a talk about physics, so this is for you."

Ell turned and strode to one end of the stage, pivoted and did handsprings toward the other end of the stage, finishing with a double and then a triple to land thunderously on the wooden stage. The audience reacted with laughter and a standing ovation as she walked back to her seat.

***

On Monday Ell got in Jake's car with him to go down to his office for his surprise. She continued to be wary about the kind of surprise Jake might have in mind, but tried hard to relax. He'd been very upbeat since she came home and they'd mended fences to the point that Ell was even staying at Jake and Kristen's house rather than her grandmother's like she usually did. His attitude had certainly changed in that he no longer implied she was ignorant, stupid, incapable or weak like he had so often intimated back in high school. He was upbeat on the trip to downtown Morehead City where his law practice dealt with real estate, fishery negotiations and other small commercial business enterprises. As they neared his office he turned to her and said, "You're really going to love the deal I've set up for you, Ell. I've worked out something better than you've *ever* dreamed of!"

Ell's blood ran cold. It sounded too much like the Jake of old. The man who always knew what was best for Ell, no matter what Ell herself wanted. "Deal?" Her voice was low and toneless and she felt bad for sounding angry before she'd even heard what was involved.

Jake, as she might have expected, didn't notice her tone. "Oh yeah! I'm not gonna say anything more. Except that you're gonna be *blown away*!"

Ell took a deep breath and forced herself to relax as they pulled into his parking space and walked into the building. She noticed it'd been remodeled since she left so he must be doing pretty well. Jake's long time receptionist, Susan, leapt out of her chair and came around to give Ell a big hug, patting her on the shoulders and welcoming her back to town. "Mr. Radford, the gentlemen are in the conference room."

Ell looked questioningly at Jake and he motioned down the little hall to where his conference room was located. When Ell entered she found two Asian men, one apparently in his 60s and the other in his 20s. They were already seated at the table. Jake thumped down into the seat across from them and said, "Sit, Ell, sit." Ell slowly slid into the seat two down from Jake and looked back and forth between Jake and the men. Jake said, "I suppose you're all wondering why I've brought you here?" then chuckled at his own little joke.

The men looked puzzled. Ell just stared at him. "So," Jake said, "Ell your worries are over. These men have come down here from Lenovo in Research Triangle Park to offer you a job. They're very interested in that paper you published in Nature. They don't feel that it's *at all* necessary that you go to grad school. They want you to start work now and I've negotiated you a starting salary of, get this, $200,000 a year!"

Ell stared at Jake, then at the two Asian men who had focused all their attention on her. She turned back to Jake and said in a flat tone, "Not interested." She started to stand.

Jake flushed. "What!" he said dangerously.

"I'm not interested in a job now. I fully intend to go to grad school, no matter how good a job might be offered to me at present. If you'd bothered to *ask*, I could have told you this at any time and saved you the trouble of setting this meeting up." She turned to the two Asian men, "I'm sorry you wasted your time coming down here."

The elder of the Asian men turned to Jake and, with a heavy accent, said icily, "I thought you said you daughter respectful and obedient?!"

Ell snorted on hearing that.

Jake's face was red and he looked like he was about to explode, but he kept his temper and ground out, "Ell, think of your mother. If you took this job you'd be able to help her out financially."

"In the first place, *you're* her husband. *You* and my mother are the ones who should depend on one another financially, not she and I. In the second, even if I were to forego grad school, I would still owe two and a half years active duty to the Air Force before I took a job."

The Asian man turned back to Jake. "Your promises were of no substance! We expect our money back."

Ell turned her icy gaze back to Jake. "How much money did you grab on the promise that I'd take this job?"

Jake opened his mouth and waved his hands defensively, but said nothing before the Asian man growled, "Two hundred thousand dollars."

Ell pointed a finger at Jake, "You owe the man his money back." She stood and opened the door.

Jake rose, "Now look here young lady!" Ell didn't hear whatever else he had to say. She'd closed the door.

She walked out front and turned brightly to Jake's receptionist. "Hey Susan, could you give me a ride home? Jake's going to be meeting with those guys a while longer."

"Sure honey, just let me get my purse."

Ell stopped at home just long enough to pack her duffle again. She slung it over her shoulder and walked to her grandmother's house. It was quite a walk, but the weather was nice. "Gram!" she said when the door opened.

Her grandmother narrowed her eyes and looked at her duffle a moment. She threw the door wide. "That S.O.B. Jake causing more trouble?"

Ell shrugged, "Yep." She said cheerfully. "Jake being Jake. *He* knows what's best for everyone."

"*Damn* that man. I don't know why Kristen stays

with him! She lets him bully her constantly. I would've thought my daughter'd have the gumption to stand up to that jackass." Gram shrugged, "Let's get you back into your old room."

~~~

Ell unpacked pensively, "Gram? I've heard of 'controlling husbands,' but never thought about it as regards Mom and Jake. I think I was oblivious to any of the signs when I lived at home. I just worried about *my* relationship with him. Do you think they've got that kind of problem?"

"Oh yeah, they've got most of the signs. I've talked to your Mom about it, but she either doesn't recognize the problem or she's too afraid to deal with it."

~~~

Ell and her grandmother talked about Kristen and Jake while they prepared and ate dinner. They had some ideas, but of course, none of their ideas would bear fruit without Kristen's initiative. Then the door creaked open and Kristen stepped in. "Ell? I thought you must be here! Why were you so rude to Jake? He said you just walked out in the middle of a presentation on the proposal he'd worked so hard to arrange!"

Gram pursed her lips. Ell stared at her mother for a moment. "Mom... Why do you think I walked out on Jake?"

Kristen looked startled, then a considering look crossed her face and she slowly sat down while looking Ell in the eye. Her face crumpled and tears ran down her cheeks, "His proposal was something he worked out completely on his own without taking your feelings into consideration at all?"

Ell slowly nodded.

"Then he said you should be grateful?" she sniffed.

Ell nodded again.

"And there was something in it for him?"

Ell leaned forward and took Kristen's hand, "Something big. You *do* know he's a controlling bully?"

Kristen looked down at the floor, wiped her nose on the back of her hand and nodded fractionally.

"Do you want our help?"

Long sobs wracked her, then she nodded. Ell and Gram both put their arms around Kristen and rocked her. "Do you want out? Or do you want to try to repair what you've got?"

"Out," she whispered.

Chapter Two

Randy idly watched the people riding down the escalator, waiting for Ell Donsaii to arrive. His eye caught on a pretty young woman riding the escalator and tracked her downward. Suddenly he realized that he was ogling the person he'd come to pick up.

~~~

Ell stepped off the escalator in the baggage area at Boston's Logan Airport and was startled when a young man approached her. At first she thought he wanted an autograph, but he said excitedly, "Ms. Donsaii, I'm Randy Dunsbaugh from MIT. Professor Golroy sent me 'round to pick you up. It's right this way to get your luggage, then we can be on our way."

Ell broke into her trademark crooked smile and held out her hand, "Ell Donsaii."

The young man seemed practically ecstatic to be shaking her hand, though he looked about twenty four and would therefore be six or seven years older than Ell. "I'm one of Professor Golroy's grad students," he enthused, "and very excited to meet you."

Randy led her to the baggage carousel. She picked up her own duffel despite the young man's attempt to get it for her. He kept up a line of chatter. "The professor's determined to have you on his theoretical team and sent me to make sure no one else horned in...

He has you set up to give a talk tomorrow at three, most of the department will be there...

I'm to warn you about Professor Smythe, one of the experimentalists. Smythe apparently thinks that you want to join an *experimental* team!"

This last about Smythe was uttered with a tone of incredulity. Apparently Randy had no idea that Ell had, in fact, requested to work in experimental physics. She was full of theories; she wanted to learn how to test them.

Randy took Ell to a nice hotel. When she protested she couldn't afford it, he assured her the Department had covered the cost. Ell was greatly relieved, but could hardly believe that they were going to this extent to woo a grad student, no matter what paper she'd written. She'd been pleased enough that they waived their requirements she take the GRE exam and that her application be submitted back last December.

And, giving a talk! "Randy, I can't give a talk! I don't have anything prepared. I've never even *heard* a talk at a physics department. I don't know what they'd expect."

"Oh, believe me, you don't have to have anything prepared. All you have to do is walk into the room and let them blast you with questions!"

"My God! That's hardly reassuring!"

"Come on! You *wrote* the paper. Surely you can answer questions about it. *No* one could know more about your new math than you do!"

***

The next day passed in a whirlwind. Randy picked

her up at the hotel and took her to breakfast with Professor Golroy. Golroy expressed his disappointment when he learned that she actually did want an experimental track in physics. However, he helped arrange appointments with Smythe and Olson, two of the faculty who *did* do experimental work with quantum phenomena.

They indeed had a conference at three, where, as promised, Ell didn't have to give a talk.

Instead, she sat with several of the professors at the front of the room. The professors on the panel asked her a series of perceptive questions at the beginning, then opened the discussion up to the room. At first Ell felt good responding to the questions, even though some were quite pointed. After all she'd worked with her math endlessly over the past couple years. She whispered to her AI, Allan, and he interfaced with computational power available on the university's servers to display graphics on the big screen at the front of the room showing how her 5th dimensional solution fit with known experimental data.

Golroy called on Dr. Josephson who'd had his hand up for a bit.

Josephson was a thin man in his early thirties. He stood up and said, "It seems to me that *all* you've done is develop your own equations that, because you made up the math you're using, happen to fit existing data? I don't see that you've predicted *anything* as yet?"

Ell's heart sank. That was *exactly* what she'd been doing. She'd thought it was pretty exciting that the equations she'd come up with fit so many known results, but put that way, it did sound like she'd just fudged things together. She considered mentioning that the equations had also fit with the results of experiments that she hadn't used when she was shaping the equations in the first place, but that felt sneaky. She really hadn't actually predicted the results of any new experiments. Heart in her mouth she cast about for something to say but nothing came to mind. She opened her mouth, then brilliantly said, "Uhhh..."

Suddenly, Dr. Smythe cleared his throat, "Josephson, you do remember that Ms. Donsaii is only seventeen years old don't you?"

Ell glanced at the balding Smythe. She'd been very impressed with his understanding of her paper when they'd interviewed earlier. Simultaneously, she felt glad that he was defending her and embarrassed that he was using her age to do it.

Josephson stiffened, "Are you suggesting that we ignore weaknesses in her theories because of her *age*?"

"You haven't found a 'weakness in her theory' you've only pointed out that it hasn't successfully predicted the result of a *new* experiment. Yet... Albert Einstein predicted phenomena that others had to test for him. Some of those predictions weren't actually successfully tested for many, many decades, many not until decades after his death. So yes, she might be wrong when her equations are tested experimentally. But she might also be right and this is *yet to be determined*. Her equations are a much better fit with existing knowledge than anything that's come along for quite some while. So, we should be eager to test predictions based on them. I'd suggest that even if her equations do fail to predict future results, you should respect the intellect that came up with those equations and a new math that fit better than anything we've had in decades. Further, you *should* respect her tender years by not jumping in her face as if she were already a grad student here and had learned to defend herself. Finally," he looked around the room, "I'd like to suggest that we *could* begin testing her math with the apparent prediction that if we entangle macromolecules such as buckyballs, we could separate them and then repeatedly perturb the distant one through her proposed 5th dimension by her predicted 'spin bumping' of outer shell electrons in the nearer member of the pair."

Smythe's proposal led to excited bickering and Ell quickly forgot Josephson's attack. Her excitement over some of the experimental testing models that were proposed had her pulse pounding. She had to do some slow deep breathing to stay out of the zone.

~~~

Ell was still ecstatic about the possible experimental methods that'd been proposed. She was daydreaming about them when she returned to her hotel. As she walked across the lobby a man with an accent called her name, "Ms. Donsaii, Ms. Donsaii."

Ell turned and saw a small Asian man wearing a dark suit trotting across the lobby toward her. "Yes?"

"Would you have a few minutes to discuss a possible scholarship for your time in graduate school here at MIT?"

She frowned, "I'm not sure I'm attending MIT."

"Or somewhere else? Mr. Chin would like to discuss the possibilities for a few moments. He's just over here in the lobby bar."

Ell just wanted to get back to her room and run some simulations on the buckyball concept. However, she really could use financial help, so she decided that she should at least listen to their offer. She turned to follow the young man, thinking it odd that two Asian groups wanted to talk to her in the same week.

She turned the corner into the bar and stopped when she saw the same older Asian man she'd encountered in Jake's office. He rose smiling and said, "Ms. Donsaii, please, I am so sorry we got off to such a bad start in Mr. Radford's office. Blame it on our Chinese preconceptions. In our country it is only polite to begin negotiations with a young woman through her parents. Won't you please listen to our offer?"

Ell grimaced, "I don't want a job. I want to learn from the best in a graduate program first."

"I understand, I understand. Mr. Radford assured us you would want a job, so that was the offer we made. But we are open to many possibilities. Presently we are thinking that you might accept financial assistance during your studies in return for consulting with us on occasion?"

"Consulting?"

"Sit, please sit. Let us offer refreshment and talk about the possibilities?"

Reluctantly, Ell sat and ordered a Coke. "What kind of consultations do you have in mind?"

Chin spoke in a rushed fashion. "We believe your new explanation for quantum phenomena has a very good chance of proving correct! Our chief scientists believe this will lead to new methods for computation. Our company wants to be at the forefront in developing products based on your theories. We would be most eager to provide you a stipend of one hundred thousand dollars per year, merely to be kept apprised of your progress and to have the right of first refusal regarding any possible products. I had my AI send a possible contract to your AI a little while ago. Did you get it?"

"Well that *would* be generous. But I have a feeling that MIT has policies in place that would compromise my freedom to sign such a document. It also might be that, even though I'm detached at present, the Air Force would also have a say in what contracts I can sign."

The younger Asian man, who'd never been introduced, came over with a Coke and set it down at Ell's elbow. Mr. Chin leaned forward conspiratorially, "We wouldn't even need a formal agreement. Just a verbal agreement to keep us apprised and we'd be happy to provide fifty thousand a year." One eyebrow rose.

Ell found this suspicious and uncomfortable. She sat back in her chair and took a long pull on her Coke. "Is this diet?" she asked, turning to the younger man.

"No it's regular Coke, why?"

"It tastes funny..."

The younger man jumped up. "I'll get them to give you another one and be sure it's regular Coke this time."

Ell took another sip and grimaced at the flavor, it just seemed off somehow. She turned back to Mr. Chin. "What's the company you work for? Lenovo?"

"Yes Ma'am."

"And that's a Chinese company, correct?"

"Yes, but we have a large presence here in the United States."

"Still, I think that the Air Force would likely object to my employment by a foreign company..." Ell realized that she *felt* funny too. She wondered if her Coke had been mixed up with someone's rum and Coke.

Mr. Chin leaned forward, "You look as if you don't

feel well, can we help you up to your room?"

"Uhhh... OK..." Ell slurred. She'd never had any alcohol. Did it work this fast?

Soon she found herself on the elevator with the two men practically holding her up. The young one pushed a button labeled "SB." "No, no; I'm up on the sixth floor..." Ell mumbled.

They didn't pay attention. She thought to herself that something bad was happening, but it somehow seemed surprisingly unimportant...

***

At ten O'clock Ell's mother Kristen tried to reach her to ask her how the interviews had gone. At first Kristen's AI said "Connecting," but then it told Kristen that Allan, Ell's AI, was off the net. Thinking that the Arab terrorists could still have reason to hate Ell, Kristen got worried and contacted Ell's hotel. Kristen persuaded the hotel to send someone up to Ell's room and to her dismay they told her that the room was unoccupied. She wondered whether there was someone at MIT she could contact to ask about Ell, but surely it would be very difficult to reach anyone at this hour of the night.

Kristen called the local police in Morehead City who were singularly unhelpful. The dispatcher said, "Her AI's battery probably went dead. You can't file a 'missing persons' report until tomorrow at the earliest."

Then Gram suggested Kristen contact Phil, "That nice young man from the Academy. He'd know what to do."

Phil was on his summer vacation in North Carolina. When they called him, he also tried to reach Ell. In view of the enemies Ell made in the terrorist group the summer before, Phil also worried that Allan's absence from the net might indicate a serious problem. He contacted Ell's friend, Chief Bowers of the Dallas Police.

Bowers actually agreed with the local police, but in view of Ell's special nature he used his police connections to obtain a warrant and download the last hour of the audio-video record from Ell's AI cameras and microphones.

The video was pretty damning, especially the drunken camera angles as Ell was maneuvered down the hall and onto the elevator. Ell's captors had unjacked her AI and turned it off as they entered the parking garage under Ell's hotel, so the record ended there. Chief Bowers contacted the Cambridge-Boston police and forwarded the record to them. Then he reluctantly called to let Ell's mom know that it appeared someone had abducted Ell.

A sobbing Kristen contacted Phil so he'd know too.

~~~

Over the next several hours Chief Bowers and the Cambridge police worked feverishly to find Ell. Ell's captors had been smart enough to turn their own AIs off before they met her in the bar to abduct her. Because of this the police weren't able to pick her captors' AIs' net addresses by their co-location in the bar where they'd drugged Ell. Facial recognition software wasn't able to match the two men recorded by Ell's AI's cameras in the hotel bar to any passports used to enter the country in the past five years. Nor had a search of rental car records turned them up. Bowers suspected they wore facial disguises, either when they entered the country and rented cars, or more likely just last night. Or might they be US citizens? The police started a search of license/ID photos, but they didn't have much luck there either.

~~~

Ell woke with a tremendous need to urinate. Her head pounded and her eyes were full of crud. When she reached up to wipe her eyes she realized her wrists were cuffed together. When she tried to get up she found her ankles were cuffed together too. She was on a bed in a dingy hotel room. The young Asian man from the bar was sleeping in a chair at the desk, his head down on his arms. "Hey," she croaked, "I've got to go to the bathroom."

The guy lifted his head, "So? Go." He dropped his head back down on the desk.

"But you've got me cuffed."

Muffled by speaking into his arms, he said, "You can still get up and shuffle to the bathroom."

Ell did so. Her cuffs were merely plastic cable ties. One around each wrist and ankle, then another loop joined the two loops on her wrists. Three loops joined the two on her ankles. The three loops made a chain between her ankles that was about ten inches long. They made it possible to shuffle, though certainly not to walk quickly. The hotel room layout was pretty standard with a bathroom next to the door into the hallway. Ell still had on her suit from the interviews, now badly rumpled. Getting her pants down was a challenge but fortunately the zipper was on the side and not in the back. She washed her hands and splashed water in her eyes. She looked in the mirror, her matted hair and bloodshot eyes looked nearly as bad as she felt. Her AI headband was gone, of course, as was the belt pack with the AI itself.

Ell looked in the medicine cabinet. Empty.

Drawers beneath the sink. Empty except for an old hand held hair dryer that looked like a fire hazard.

No window in the bathroom. Vinyl floor, tile walls. The bathtub-shower combo had a mildewed curtain over it, but otherwise nothing in it. Ell lifted the top off the tank of the toilet—nothing but a standard flapper and float valve setup. She stepped to the bathroom door, unlocked and opened it, looking out, "Hey, I need a toothbrush!"

Without lifting his head he said, "It's the middle of the night! Go back to sleep!"

Ell figured that they'd drugged her at about nine PM. If the drugs didn't keep her asleep longer than her usual three or four hours, then it must be a little after midnight. Partly for information and partly to irritate her keeper she asked, "What time is it?"

With a moan, he said, "The middle of the damned night!"

Ell realized that her short sleep cycle represented an advantage. "I need a Tylenol or an aspirin."

"You aren't getting either, *go* back to sleep!"

Ell looked around the room for a weapon she could use with her hands bound together. There was a lamp, but it was on the desk where the man's head rested. "What do you and Mr. Chin think you're going to do with me anyway?" She leaned out to look at the man, raising a querying eyebrow.

"Go back to bed!"

Ell shuffled over to the small closet on the other side of the short hall from the bathroom and opened it. *Ah, wire coat hangers and a wooden hanger rod!* Ell looked at the bed, a simple double mattress. Light fixtures and night stands bolted to the wall behind it. Small dresser with a cheap monitor screen across from the bed. She shuffled to the dresser and pulled the drawers out, throwing them on the floor with a loud clatter.

The man raised his head and stared at her, "*What* are you *doing*?"

"Looking for my AI."

"Your AI isn't in here. Get some sleep! Mr. Chin will explain everything in the morning. We just need your help for a while, then we'll release you."

"I don't feel tired. Help with what?"

"If you don't lie down I'll attach your cuffs to the bed."

Ell shuffled across the room to look out the window. It looked out at the brick wall of the next building, which was only about two feet away! These were some *fine* accommodations. She shuffled back over to the bed and sat down. "Happy?"

"Yes." He started to lower his head to the desk.

"What's your name?"

He rolled his eyes. "Call me Mr. Chang."

"Chin and Chang?"

"Not our real names."

"First name?"

"Chang."

Ell flopped back on the bed and thought about what she'd learned. Her self-defense courses at the Academy had taught that escape was easiest at the beginning of captivity. The longer you gave your captor, the more secure he could make your imprisonment. She considered what she had to work with. She stretched and flopped over so her feet hung off the bathroom-closet side of the bed. Her head was feeling better. She sat back up and turned. "Chang?"

Laurence E Dahners

With a groan, "Yeah."

"You know I'm dangerous right?"

"Yes," he ground out, "But, you're bound hand and foot. I'm armed. I have backup in the next room. They're watching you through my AI's cameras. *Please* don't try anything; we really *don't* want to hurt you."

"That's reassuring. I don't want to hurt you either." Ell, took a few deep breaths to suppress a surge of adrenalin that might have put her in the zone prematurely. Then she got up and shuffled off to the bathroom.

"Where are you going now?

"Thirsty, want a drink."

Ell was relieved to see Chang put his head back down as she turned into the bathroom. She shut the door and pressed the latch button. She turned on the water, opened the drawer and pulled out the ancient hair dryer, inspecting it. The plastic casing was already cracked. She banged her hip into the counter at the same time as she slammed the dryer's case against the sink. The case shattered.

Ell picked at the remaining shell as she responded to Chang's query. "I tripped on these damned ankle cuffs! Can't you take them off?"

"No! Open the door!"

Ell placed the dryer back in the drawer and shut it, kicked fragments of its case back behind the toilet, then turned off the water and opened the door, holding her head as if it were hurt and raising her eyebrows at him in query.

Chang looked around the bathroom suspiciously but then went back out to his desk.

Ell relocked the door, jammed a piece of plastic from the case into the fan of the hair dryer and plugged it in.

In a minute the heating element was red hot. She hopped up on the sink to hold one of the cable ties between her ankle cuffs against the coil of red hot wire. To her relief the strap melted quickly, creating only a little smoke that the bathroom fan quickly carried away. Next she held the handle of the dryer between her knees and melted off her right and left wrist cuffs. Chang still hadn't noticed what she was doing so she melted the cuffs off each of her ankles too.

Ell unplugged the drier and ran her fingers through her hair while she thought a moment. Then she stepped across the hall to the closet. She lifted the 24 inch wooden hanger bar off its support and dumped the hangers into the corner.

Chang, roused by the clatter of the hangers, jumped up and was coming her way when she stepped back from the closet, her right hand grasping the hanger rod, but hiding it behind the open door. She let her adrenalin spike and felt the zone crash over her. The world slowed and her heart beat became a ponderous throb. Knowing she was moving so fast that speaking at what felt like an ordinary speed to her would be too fast for Chang to understand, she slowly said, "Put, your, hands, up!"

Chang stared at Ell's wrist, realized her hand was free and started scrabbling his hand into his coat. Ell, feeling like she had all the time in the world, stepped fully back from the closet and then toward him, the hanger bar already whistling up from down low, making an arc toward his hands. As a gun cleared his lapel, the hanger bar struck Chang's hand, traveling upward so it drove the muzzle up. It ripped the weapon out of his hand and flung it against the ceiling. As the gun fell from the ceiling, Ell stepped over to catch it, then back to Chang who was beginning to crouch and cradle his fractured hand. Speaking slowly to help him understand, she said, "Sorry, but, I, *did,* remind, you I'm, dangerous."

She pulled his AI headband off his head and jerked the cable out of the belt pack. She examined his gun, a Smith and Wesson, found the safety, worked the slide to chamber a round and put the gun in her waistband. She stepped into the bathroom, tossed Chang's AI headband into the toilet and grabbed the hair dryer. She jerked the cord loose from the hairdryer's handle, noting with satisfaction that it came out with bare wire exposed. Ell put the plug back in the wall and touched one of the wires to the spigot. This produced a heavy spark that dropped the GFI and darkened the bathroom, identifying the hot wire. She unplugged the cord. She took it into the entryway hall where she hung one of the bare wire coat hangers over the doorknob. She twisted the active wire from the hair dryer cord onto the coat hanger and plugged the cord into the hall outlet which wasn't GFI protected. Just as she stepped away she saw the knob jiggle then heard a loud thump. Whoever'd grasped the knob had been shocked off his feet.

~~~

Chang, still holding his injured right hand in his left, stood back up, determined to do something to stop this madwoman. *She moves unbelievably fast,* he thought, *I wonder what made the deep electric buzz while she was in the bathroom.*

She strode his way so he reached out toward her with his good hand.

She grabbed the wooden hanger bar and sent it

whistling through the air to slam into his shin. As he fell she said, "Sorry, can't have you following me."

~~~

Ell had started toward the window intending to use rock climbing techniques to climb down the "chimney" between her building and the next. She stopped when someone kicked the door hard. With some irritation she realized that her door knob shocker wouldn't keep them from *kicking* the door in. She turned back, pivoted the switched-off monitor screen on the dresser toward the door, then stepped over to stand against the wall between the room and the bathroom. As she'd hoped, she could see the entry door faintly reflected in the monitor. More crashes came from the door, then it broke open. A young Asian man rushed in, followed by Mr. Chin, both of them holding pistols.

Ell could faintly see someone lying in the hallway outside. She hoped the shock hadn't killed him.

The first man's pistol passed the corner and she struck him on the wrists with the hanger bar. Then she stepped around the corner, knocked Chin's pistol aside with the wooden rod and punched him in the solar plexus.

Chin doubled over gasping. She took the pistol out of his hand and turned back to the first man. He backed warily away from her, cradling his broken wrists one in another. "Where's my AI?" she asked. The man just shook his head at her. "Where's my AI?" she said, trying to sound threatening and raising the hanger rod. His eyes widened but he just shook his head some more.

Chang gritted out, "He doesn't speak much English. Your AI's probably in the next room."

"Tell him I'm going to pat him down."

Chang said something that sounded like Chinese to Ell. She stepped over and patted the man down and went through his pockets. She found a plastic room key, a bundle of cable ties, and two magazines of ammunition for his gun but nothing else.

She looked at the three men, none looked threatening at the moment. Chin was still gasping for breath. She thought he should recover in another minute. The man in the hall moaned and rolled over. *Still alive*, she thought.

Ell let herself to come down out of the zone. She took off her rumpled suit coat, then collected their AIs and guns, stacking them on her jacket. Ell bent over Chin, using three cable ties to bind his wrists together and three more to bind his ankles. She went through his pockets, finding them empty. She dragged the guy in from the hall, checked his pockets and bound him, then the other two. Guns, ammunition and room keys were all she found on them.

She turned back to their stacked weapons. They were all 9mm Smith and Wessons. She quickly familiarized herself with them, ejecting the magazines, racking the slides and then tossing all the ammunition in the toilet except the mag in the gun in her waistband. She carried her jacket with the AIs and guns out into the hall and tried the men's room keys, finding that they opened the room across the hall and the one next door. Searching the first room she found her AI in a drawer, booted it and put it on. Ell began searching the men's luggage. She only found wallets and IDs for four men, Chin, Chang, Wong and Lau, hopefully suggesting that there weren't more of their team about to show up.

Allan chimed in her earpiece and said, "Ready. You have messages."

Ell said, "Please contact Chief Bowers of the Dallas police."

Ell resumed her search. There was clothing and more ammunition, but little else to explain the Chinese men's mission or what they'd intended to do with Ell.

Chief Bowers' voice sounded in her ear, "Ell? Where are you?" He sounded wide awake despite the late hour.

"Sorry to wake you up in the middle of the night Chief, but I'm wanting to take you up on your offer of help if I ever needed it."

"You aren't waking me up. We've been trying to find you! What's happened?" He sounded apprehensive.

"I've been visiting MIT and some men who appear to be Chinese nationals drugged me and tried to kidnap me. They apparently wanted me to do some quantum physics work for them, even though I haven't had any training yet. I just escaped a few minutes ago."

"My God! That's what the last feed from your AI looked like. We couldn't figure out why the Chinese would be kidnapping you. We were all thinking they might be working for your Arab terrorist friends. Are you safe with the Cambridge police?"

"Well... That's what I'm calling about. I haven't contacted the police yet and I'm hoping you'll run interference with them for me so this doesn't get overblown in the news?"

"Haven't contacted them!? Are you in a safe location?"

"Well... All four of my attackers are disabled and cuffed. I'm staying with them so far. Shouldn't I stay with them, at least until the police arrive?"

The chief choked out a laugh. "I guess I forgot who I was talking to. I don't know what they were thinking, taking Ell Donsaii on without an entire army to back them up. I've had my AI start re-contacting the Boston-Cambridge area police so I can brief them on your situation, but first describe it to me in more detail."

Ell told him what she knew. Allan, Ell's AI, confirmed that she'd been in their hands for about five hours, but Allan's GPS said Ell was now about 120 miles from Boston, in Hartford, Connecticut, at the Berford Arms Hotel. The chief took Ell's room number and said he'd get back to her once he'd reached the police in Hartford.

Ell continued her search of the rooms without finding anything else of significance. While she searched she listened to a series of more and more frantic messages from her mother, then Phil, then Chief Bowers, then the Cambridge police. Listening to the messages, she was touched that so many people had made such efforts on her behalf. To Ell's amazement Phil's last message said he was currently waiting at the RDU airport in Raleigh for the next plane to Boston! Ell said, "Allan, call Mom."

Kristen's voice came on breathlessly, "Ell! Are you OK? Chief Bowers said you were kidnapped!"

"I'm OK now. They drugged me, but I escaped. The police should be here soon. Don't worry too much and try to get some sleep. I'm still hoping to catch my scheduled flight back to RDU in the morning."

"You escaped? Are they still looking for you?"

"No, they're all in handcuffs. I'm keeping an eye on them until the police arrive to take custody." Ell talked to her mom a little longer but hung up as soon as Kristen seemed calm.

She said, "Allan, call Phil."

Phil sounded sleepy when he said, "Ell?"

"Hey, I'm OK. I escaped. Thanks for helping my mom last night."

"You escaped? Damn!"

Ell snorted, "What, you *wanted* me in captivity?"

"No! But I was looking forward to rescuing *you* for a change. You can't imagine how embarrassing it is for a big guy like me to have l'il ol' you save my ass twice."

"Well boyo, sorry to disappoint you, but I guess you're just gonna have to wait til next time to rescue me. Hey, your message said you're at the airport in Raleigh waiting to fly up to Boston, but I'm going to fly back down to RDU in the morning. Maybe I can buy you lunch for your trouble?" Ell's heart leaped into her throat. She felt like she'd just asked him on a date or something. She really liked the big hunk and would love to go out with him, but worried the feeling wasn't reciprocated. She steeled her heart against a sudden expectation of rejection.

To Ell's relief Phil responded enthusiastically, "It's a date! Just let me know when your plane's arriving?"

The police arrived, so Ell had to hang up. But the words, "It's a date," rolled happily around in her head.

The Hartford police took custody of "Chin, Chang, Wong and Lau." After interrogating Ell's and Chang's AIs they took a statement corroborating the record on the AIs from Ell and released her. When they learned she was scheduled for a Boston to Raleigh flight in the morning, they assigned one of their young officers to deliver her back to Logan Airport.

As Ell was about to leave the senior officer stopped her. "Ms. Donsaii?"

"Yes sir?"

"We've been interrogating Chin's AI and its records showed they'd arranged a charter flight leaving

Newark's Liberty Airport tomorrow afternoon. These guys were very serious about taking you somewhere *far* out of our jurisdiction. I'd strongly urge you to be very, very careful."

Heart sinking Ell said morosely, "Yes sir."

~~~

Riding in the police cruiser on the way back to Boston, Ell had time to think about the implications of what'd just happened. These people wanted her, and they had tremendous resources. Somehow, she didn't think their failure this time would scare them off. Ell got depressed just thinking about them coming after her again and again. How would she protect herself from eventual capture by a group that had the kind of assets this one did? Sure, she'd been able to escape this time, but next time they might just *keep* her drugged until they had her on foreign soil. She sighed.

The young officer riding in the driver's seat said, "Hey, what's got you so down? That was amazing, the way you got away from those guys back there."

"I just have the feeling that someone else is going try the same thing. Maybe I won't get away next time."

"Hmmpf, you should get into witness protection or something. If they didn't know who or where you were, they wouldn't be able to track you down."

"Really?" Ell's eyebrows rose at the thought, "Do you think I could?"

"Well, I have an aunt down in North Carolina who could help you with the disguise part. The real problem is getting permission to legally use another name. That can be a big hassle. But you seem to know some big names in the police hierarchy; I'll bet they could make it happen for you."

As Ell was pondering this Allan said, "Call from Chief Bowers."

"Answer."

"Ell?" She heard the chief say.

"Yes?"

"I understand you're in transit back to the airport in Boston to catch your flight?"

"Yes, they've been kind enough to send me back in a police cruiser. Probably due to your influence. Thanks so much!"

"Well the Hartford police also told me disturbing things about the group that kidnapped you. They were obviously planning to take you out of the country in the morning and then it would've been *hell* trying to find you! They had extensive assets available to them, possibly even national resources from the PRC."

"If you're trying to make me even more depressed, Chief, you're succeeding. Do you have any ideas what I can do to keep them from succeeding next time?"

"Next time? These guys are going up the river. There won't be any next time... Oh... you figure that whoever sent this group will probably send an even bigger team after this one failed?"

"Yeah. Do you think they'll have been dissuaded? Or that the police can track down whoever sent them and apply pressure somehow?"

"Hmm, you may be right. We might be able to find out who sent them, but we might not. Even if we do, we might not be able to bring effective influence to bear. Maybe if the President got involved?"

"I don't want to start asking the *President* for favors! Officer Galway, who's taking me back to Boston, suggested I should get into Witness Protection. Do you think that's possible? I'd kinda like not being recognized and pestered for autographs all the time."

"I'm not sure; you're not a witness after all. I'll check with our folks who do that kind of thing in the morning. I'll let you get back to trying to get some sleep on your ride to Boston. But you be careful till we work something out. I'd try to get you assigned some police protection," he snorted, "but I'd be afraid you'd wind up protecting *them*."

Galway also suggested Ell try to get some sleep, but she'd already had almost four hours of sleep, plenty for her. She reclined the seat and pretended to sleep while trying to work on her quantum theory again. Thinking about quantum theory usually calmed her, but her thoughts kept wandering off onto what would happen when she saw Phil the next day.

Will he actually show up? she wondered.

Chapter Three

As her plane left Boston, Ell sent Phil a message that she was on her way. Then she fidgeted and worried the entire flight about whether he'd actually be there. Was lunch with an old friend all he was interested in? He'd been cool and standoffish for so long after they got started on the wrong foot, three years ago now. He'd thawed this last year, but at the Academy the rules forbade them from considering each other as possible boyfriend or girlfriend material.

Now that I'm out, might he be interested?

Am I just infatuated with his amazing physical condition?

Is he still afraid of me?

Right after the terrorist stuff at the Olympics he said he'd be happy to be my boyfriend—did he mean it? If so, does that still apply?

When she got down to baggage claim, Phil was standing there, all big and blond and Norse God looking. *Damn, the man looks as good as ever!* A grin split his face and he stepped over and wrapped her in his arms.

So much for whether he'd be friendly.

He squeezed and she squeaked, then he held her out at arm's length, "Hey! You look good. I spent some serious time wondering if I'd ever see you again."

Ell grinned crookedly up at him for a moment, then with a serious look she said, "Hey, thanks for looking out for me. I know my mother really appreciated your help."

"Well, I didn't do much. But I'm hungry, so I'm ready to have you buy me lunch for anything I might have done."

"Much more importantly than what you did, I appreciate what you were willing to do. I can't believe you were going to fly up to Boston and look for me!"

"Hah! You're my classmate! Of course I'd do whatever I could to pull your ass out of the fire…" he looked down, "Well, I guess you aren't actually my classmate anymore…"

Feeling a little hurt to be just a classmate, Ell asked in a small voice, "Can I be your friend instead?"

"Always! Well," he mused, "except for when I'm remembering that you're the only one to ever really kick my ass in a fight…"

Ell punched him gently in the arm, "Someday you're going to *have* to forgive me for that." She tried to sound timid, "I was scared."

Phil looked down at the floor and scuffed a toe, "Jus' not right, fifteen year old girl beatin' up a full grown man… Jus' not right."

Ell playfully punched him again, then grabbed her duffle and they headed off to lunch. There they talked about her kidnapping and escape and whether the Chinese would really have another crack at capturing her? Ell kept hoping the conversation would stray back toward their relationship, but Phil focused entirely on her situation and what they could do about it. He thought witness protection was a great idea, but that it was sad she might have to stoop to disguising herself.

Long after they'd finished their hamburgers and been asked repeatedly and eventually, pointedly, by the waitress if they "needed anything else?" they finally got up and left. Ell left a painfully big tip when she paid for their lunch. Phil walked her to Ell's mom's car which had driven up to get her. For a moment she thought he might give her another hug or even, maybe, a kiss?

But he just shook her hand and slapped the roof of the car as it pulled away.

~~~

As Ell's car rolled away, Phil shook his head. Why didn't I at least give her another hug? Damn it, I *like* the girl! I can't still be afraid of her can I? *Although*, he thought, *just about anybody with any common sense would be afraid of her.*

~~~

Ell huddled down in the seat of the car and swallowed around the lump in her throat. *It was great to see Phil. Why am I so sad?*

~~~

After a few minutes on the road Ell's AI said in her earpiece, "Dr. Smythe from MIT is calling."

Ell's voice croaked a little, "Yes?"

"Ell, we were extremely impressed yesterday and we'd very much like to offer you a position as a graduate student in our program." He paused for a moment, "Are you OK? Your voice sounds kind of ragged."

Ell cleared her throat. "Uh, yes sir. I'm fine." She pondered a moment about whether to tell Smythe what had happened, then decided honesty was best. "It's been a little stressful. I was kidnapped last night by a group that apparently thought they could force me to work on my quantum theories for them."

Laurence E Dahners

"What! My God! I assume that you were rescued or I wouldn't be talking to you, but where were they going to take you?"

"Out of the country. They had a plane chartered out of Newark's Liberty Airport. Probably to China since they all appeared to be Chinese."

"Were they captured? Are you safe now?"

"Yeah, they were captured and I'm probably safe from *them*. But, if they were supported by a sovereign state, I'm worried such a country might just send other operators."

"That's terrible! Do you have police protection?"

"Well, not right now. And they might not come after me again for months; I don't think the police'd be willing to follow me around for the years that it'd take to actually be effective in preventing another attempt."

"My God! Are there any other plans for how to keep you safe? Is there anything *I* can do?"

"We're talking about something like witness protection, where I'd be disguised and assume another identity to throw them off."

"Oh! I guess that might work. I'm sure I could work it out so that we could admit you under an alias."

"I'm… I'm worried that, since they kidnapped me in Cambridge, MIT's the first place they'd look for me, even if I *were* in a disguise. I hate to ask, but could you help me with references for my alias at another institution?"

"Ouch! You *really* don't think you could work with us here?"

"Maybe? Depending on what they find out about my kidnappers."

"Well, if you do have to go into hiding, I have a experimental physics friend right in your home state,

North Carolina. I could talk to him for you. He's an irascible SOB, but he's really good at experimental studies of quantum phenomena. I can probably even exert some influence with him to take you." Smythe paused for a moment, then said, "Even if you're in hiding, I'd hope that some means for me to talk to you about your theories could still be set up?"

"Oh yeah! I'd *really* like that."

They spoke a little longer on inconsequential matters. When Ell hung up she started thinking about physics with some excitement again.

Allan said, "You have a call from Chief Bowers."

"I'll take it...Yes Chief?"

"Hello Ell. I've just finished talking to the U.S. Marshal's office and they agree you could be a candidate for witness protection if you're willing to testify against the people who kidnapped you?"

"Sure!"

"OK, I've made you an appointment to meet with the Marshals' office in Raleigh tomorrow morning."

"Achhh! I'm just driving home from Raleigh now. But, sure, I'll be back tomorrow morning, just have them send me a time and location."

***

The next morning Ell walked into the Federal building on New Bern Avenue in Raleigh. After a brief search she found the Marshal's office and she was introduced to Gloria Sanchez, a Witness Protection specialist.

Ms. Sanchez said, "Normally, when we have someone come into witness protection we plan on their 'becoming someone else' and never returning to their original identity, but I'm betting that you still want to be 'Ell Donsaii' sometimes?"

"Oh, *yes* Ma'am. Is that going to be a problem?"

"You bet it is. Every time you show up as 'Ell Donsaii' there's a chance someone will trace you back and compromise your new identity. I'd *really* recommend against maintaining two identities, but this is a free country. I can tell you not to do it, but there's nothing to keep you from going against my advice."

"Well, I'll try to keep it to a minimum. Would you be able to give me advice on how to lose tails when I'm about to change from one identity to another?"

"Sure," Sanchez said reluctantly. With a sigh she commenced a description of measures Ell could take.

The next thing was to work on her new identity and its necessary documentation. They sat down to pick out a name.

"Can I pick a name myself?"

Gloria said, "Sure, but I think it's better if we pick a name you'll notice if someone calls out to you by your new name. Something like 'Ellen Symonds,' which I really like because the first and last names share syllables with your real name. That means that if someone calls out to you, you're more likely to take note and respond correctly."

"Ellen Symonds." Ell said, trying the name out for feel.

"Ell Donsaii, Ellen Symonds. Close but not too close."

"OK."

"Good, let me talk to Jim about getting the documentation started and I'll be right back."

While she was gone, Ell thought about how weird it was going to be, going by a new name. She said the name over and over in her mind, trying to get used to it.

Gloria came back in. "Let me have you stand up so I can look at you and we can think about disguising you." After Ell stood Gloria had her turn around several times. She asked, "Any thoughts on how you want to look?"

"Not really. My current look attracts a lot of unwanted attention from men."

Gloria smirked, "You think you're *too* cute?!"

"Well… kinda," Ell blushed, "I hope that doesn't sound stuck up?"

"No, I just never thought I'd have a woman ask me to make her less attractive." Gloria snorted, "I thought our genes were hardwired against such requests."

"Well, you don't need to make me look hideous."

Gloria leaned back and rubbed her chin, "Hmmm. Your slender build gives us a lot more options. I suggest we disguise your body with some padded underwear to make your hips and butt bigger. You'll have to buy some larger pants and skirts. Then you'll wear tight sports bras all the time to make your top appear smaller. That combo alone will significantly reduce the attention guys give you. Skin bronzers to make your coloring darker and we can darken your hair too. Finally we'll change your nose a little."

"Wow! All that?"

"Sure, no half measures."

They searched the Net together and ordered some padded underpants in Ell's size. They were to be delivered to Gloria. No disguise materials should be delivered to any of Ell's addresses. For now they tucked some pieces of a torn up t-shirt into the pants Ell had on.

Gloria took Ell in the bathroom and moussed her hair into a spiky do with a mousse that immediately darkened her reddish-blond hair to dark brunette. They applied a soluble bronzer to all of Ell's exposed skin, though Gloria told Ell she'd need to do the rest of her skin when she got home so pale areas couldn't be accidentally exposed, giving her away. Then Gloria took a mold of Ell's nose and built a silicone bump for it, carefully coloring it to match her new darker skin tone. She skin glued it in place and then showed Ell how to apply makeup to conceal it. Gloria had to teach Ell a lot about makeup since Ell had rarely worn any. She'd need to wear a moderate amount to make this disguise work.

When Gloria was done, Ell looked in the mirror in astonishment. She hadn't dreamed a disguise this good would be possible. Gone was the reddish-blond girl of northern European descent. In her place was a swarthy Middle Eastern woman with a hooked nose and a spiky butch hairdo who was definitely bottom heavy. Ell wasn't enamored of the new look, but had to admit she hardly recognized herself. She'd always thought that she wasn't vain, but she found the big bottom and the nose a little bit embarrassing. *Well, you thought it would be nice if men didn't stare at you so much!* she thought to herself with some chagrin. *Problem solved!*

She chuckled.

Gloria said, "What are you laughing about?"

Ell just shook her head and gave Gloria an embarrassed grin, "I'd rather not say."

~~~

When she got home later that afternoon, Ell drove directly to the seaside diner where her mother waited tables in the summer and went in to take a seat in her mother's section. Her mother came over with a menu. Per Gloria's instruction she pitched her voice a little higher than usual and used her best imitation of a nasal New York accent to order a cherry Coke and an order of French fries. Ell noticed her mother couldn't suppress a slight frown of disapproval regarding her nutritional choices. Nonetheless, Ell felt gratified that even her own mother didn't seem to recognize her.

~~~

When Ell's mother arrived back at Gram's house she was startled to see the girl from the diner sitting at the table. "Hello, um, what are you doing here?"

"Hi Mom, thought I'd sleep here tonight."

"Ell!?"

"Yup, the disguise lady's pretty good, huh?"

"My God!" Kristen stared at her daughter for a moment, then narrowed her eyes and put her hands on her hips. "A Coke and fries for lunch?!"

~~~

The next few weeks were a whirlwind. Ell's Mom and Jake were separated as required by North Carolina law prior to getting divorced. Ell provided emotional support wherever she could.

Ell practiced her New York accent until it became almost natural. Soon she could turn it off and on effortlessly. She practiced putting her nose prosthetic and makeup on until it became a quick, second nature task. She never again appeared as Ellen Symonds outside the house in Morehead City though.

Ell drove to Raleigh and picked up the permanent parts of her disguise from Gloria as well as documentation for "Ellen Symonds." This included a New York birth certificate, passport, social security card, driver's license, college transcript from UVA and faked results for the SAT. Ell felt startled to see she was suddenly old enough to drink. Special software was installed on Allan, her AI so that he had a divided personality, Allan for her old life and "Fred" for Ellen Symonds. Gloria had similar software on her AI, allowing her to serve as Ellen's widowed mother and only surviving relative should anyone try to contact Ellen Symonds' family.

~~~

While she was in Raleigh she interviewed at NCSU's physics department with Dr. Al Johnson. Dr. Johnson was the friend that Dr. Smythe had recommended her to.

"It's *very* late to be interviewing for a spot as a graduate assistant Ms. Symonds. If it weren't for the good things that Dr. Smythe had to say about you, we wouldn't even be talking."

"Yes sir. I'm sorry, but I've had some traumatic events in my life that made it impossible for me to go to MIT like I'd planned." It wasn't quite true that Ell had planned to go to MIT, but Dr. Smythe had actually suggested the fib to Ell as a way to cover the fact that she should have applied to NCSU long ago.

"What happened?"

"I'm sorry, I really can't talk about it."

"Hmmpf. That's what Smythe said. I really don't like taking you on without even knowing what happened to your spot at MIT."

"I'm so sorry. If you don't feel you can offer me a spot without the full application process, I guess I'll just have to apply next year?"

"No, no. Smythe assures me that I'll be sorry if I don't take you on. I don't know what he sees in your record that makes him think you're going to be some kind of superstar."

"I'm not sure either sir. I do hope I can live up to his, and of course, your expectations."

He snorted, "Can't even answer that one, eh? OK, I'll bite. I'm intrigued enough by the expectations Smythe has that I'll invest *some* time in you. But, I warn you now, if you don't live up to my expectations, you'll get the boot so fast your head'll spin, understood?"

"Yes sir." Ell said quietly, not sure she liked Johnson. She wondered once again whether if she could feel safe at MIT in her new disguise? Smythe was *so* much nicer! Of course MIT also had Dr. Josephson who she hadn't liked, but at least she wouldn't have had to work with Josephson one on one.

"OK," Johnson said, "I'll talk to the admin secretary about getting you admitted and your AI should get something about it soon. You'll be expected to teach one lab for my elementary physics class but, mostly you'll be working in the research program." He shook his head, "I hope you're as good as Smythe thinks you are."

"Yes sir."

"I'm going to assign you some prep work. Smythe says you're interested in that crazy paper by Donsaii, that gymnast?"

Ell felt goose bumps on her neck. "Yes sir, I've been very interested."

"Well, personally, I think her theory's a load of crap. This math the girl invented is beyond bizarre. Even if she has successfully massaged it until it fits with current experimental data, the chances that it will correctly *predict* anything are microscopic."

Ell's heart sank as she heard this appraisal, but

Johnson hadn't asked for a comment so she didn't respond.

Johnson went on, "But, *that* is what we experimentalists do. We test crazy predictions by hare brained theorists *just in case* one of them's actually correct. Personally, I'm going to enjoy proving that this 'wunderkind gymnast' is an idiot. She's gotten entirely too much attention at *way* too young an age. Probably thinks her crap doesn't stink like everyone else's."

He'd paused, so, in a small voice, Ell said, "Yes sir."

"All that aside, for you to be able to do experiments on her predictions, you're going to have to understand her math backwards and forwards. So, in your spare time the rest of this summer, get yourself chin deep in that paper she wrote and learn how to work her math for actual testable predictions. Smythe thinks that the 'low hanging fruit' for a testable hypothesis is her absurd prediction that you can 'spin bump' an entangled molecule's outer shell electrons and measure an instantaneous 'quiver' in the electrons of the distant molecule of the entangled pair."

Amused to be told she had to study a paper she'd written herself, Ell nonetheless said, "Yes sir." with a straight face.

"Unfortunately, 'spin bumping' is a hypothesis that might be possible to prove correct *if* it worked. But, when it *doesn't* work we won't be able to be sure that was because the theory is hogwash. There'll still be the possibility that the 'spin bumping' apparatus we came up with didn't work right. So, what I want you to do is look for other testable hypotheses that'll be easier to prove wrong."

"Yes sir." Ell said quietly, trying not to show how disappointed she felt that she might not be allowed to try to prove that spin bumping worked.

"Now, starting out, you don't know squat about experimental methods, so you'll have to talk to me about what you think her theory predicts would happen and I'll help you figure out whether we *can* test it. I suppose we'll have to make a few runs at this 'spin bumping' crap too. Even though I think it'll be complete waste of time, it *will* be good practice for you in setting up apparatus."

"Yes sir." Ell said, feeling slightly cheered.

"OK, head on over to admin, they should know about you by the time you get there." He turned back to his screens without shaking her hand or saying goodbye.

"Yes sir." Ell got up and left, not at all sure she wanted to work with the man. Maybe she could transfer somewhere else after a semester?

***

Hands on his hips, Li looked critically around the basement of the house his team had rented in Goldsboro, North Carolina. "OK, it'll have to do. We need desks to work at and some large monitor screens. Set up cameras at her father's and grandmother's houses in Morehead City and at the arrival areas in the RDU and ILM airports. At the airports we'll have to rely on facial recognition software, but at her homes I want one of us to inspect the image of every person who comes or goes.

"Hao, you drive the roads here and in Morehead City until you know them as well as your own hometown.

"Xian, rent us a house on the barrier island with a

dock. Then rent a boat to put in that dock and practice taking the boat out to the various rendezvous points.

"Cho, you will obtain weapons, a net jammer, and equipment to immobilize her. I know she's 'just a girl,' but remember that she dealt successfully with those Arab terrorists. More importantly think about the fact how the team that preceded us was *captured* themselves while trying to remove her from the country.

"We will over-plan and over-prepare. We will *not* fail like Chin."

Chapter Four

While she was at home over the summer, Ell found herself constantly looking over her shoulder, especially when she encountered people of Asian extraction.

When she registered at NCSU in August, her feelings of sadness at leaving home again were mixed with quite a bit of excitement to begin testing her theories and significant relief that, as Ellen Symonds, she no longer felt she had to worry much about kidnappers.

Reading the syllabus she decided that setting up labs for the introductory physics class looked like it'd be fun. When she reported to Dr. Johnson's office on her first day, he walked her down the hall to introduce her to another grad student. "Ellen Symonds, This is Roger Emmerit, he's worked in the lab for three years now, so he can show you the ropes. I'll see you at the lab meeting this afternoon at 3." Johnson turned and left without saying good bye.

Ell found herself staring at Johnson's retreating back. Roger cleared his throat. Ell turned back to the tall young man. Wearing jeans and running shoes, he had a bushy shock of dark hair standing straight up. Ell wondered if he was cultivating Einstein's wild haired look. The look seemed to fit him, creating a wild, but improbably, a somewhat exotically handsome appearance.

~~~

For his part, Roger was looking askance at the odd looking young woman Johnson'd left in his charge. He thought to himself that she could be cute if she didn't have such a beak of a nose. And her tummy and backside were way big for his taste. *Too bad she doesn't work out a little.* He said, "Don't worry; Johnson's bark's worse than his bite. I hear he wants you to work on that crazy paper by Donsaii?"

Ell grimaced internally, "Yes sir."

"Don't 'sir' me, I work for a living… Uh, that's what my dad always said. He was a sergeant in the Marines."

"OK… But, uh yes, I *am* to work on Donsaii's ideas and see if we can test any of her predictions."

"Oh Jeez, I *feel* for you. When you're trying to prove something and it doesn't work, critics always blame your deficient experimental setup."

"What if we *do* confirm some of her predictions?"

"Hah! Have you read her paper yet? Fat chance on that one. This math she's proposed is incomprehensible! I mean she's undoubtedly some kind of genius to work out a math that *seems* to correlate with existing results, but I can't believe there's any way it's gonna work for future predictions. Actually, I'd love it if she turned out to be right, but this stuff she's proposing is just too counterintuitive."

~~~

At the 3PM lab meeting that day Johnson quizzed each of his grad students about their research progress. When he got to Ell he said, "So, do you understand the math in that paper?"

"I believe so sir."

"Believe?"

Smarter

"Sir, I *do* understand it," Ell said, trying to project confidence with her second answer.

"OK, if you understand it, then explain that second equation that purports to show how entangled but separated particles can connect through this 5th dimension of hers."

Ell took a deep breath and had her AI throw up the equation on the wall screen, then began solving it as two manifestations of a particle were separated farther and farther in physical space, demonstrating that, using the conventions of her own math, the particles could remain connected through an additional fifth dimension.

~~~

Roger listened in growing astonishment as Ellen responded to question after question thrown at her by Johnson. At any moment he expected her to break. He'd seen a lot of other grad students crumble under a less punishing barrage of questions than the one Johnson was pounding her with. She not only didn't get flustered, she answered every question as if she'd already considered it herself. Johnson was asking them in a very pointed fashion, readily showing his doubt that she'd be able to answer. At first Johnson almost seemed frustrated that she didn't stumble, and then seemed to be listening carefully to her explanations, almost as if she was the teacher and he the student. Roger's opinion of the young woman skyrocketed. He'd been thinking of her as a clueless new grad student with an impossible assignment, but if she could actually understand Donsaii's math this thoroughly and this quickly she *had to be* be pretty smart!

It's a shame she's got a project with so little chance

of success, he thought to himself.

"Well?" Johnson rasped, "You do realize that this 'spin bumping,' if true, would violate relativity?"

"Yes sir. If it worked, you'd be able to transmit, information at least, essentially instantaneously. Uh, I assume that you are referring to the fact that that would be faster than the speed of light and *thus* violate relativity?"

"Yes, and relativity has stood up to a lot of testing in the past. It hasn't even quivered."

"Um, yes sir. But, because the purported fifth dimension is small, distances within it are tiny and therefore information transmission there can be slow and still appear to be faster than light in the dimensions we're aware of."

Johnson grunted, "That is *so* unlikely you'd just as well buy tickets for the lottery. Are you *sure* you want to beat your head on that wall?"

"Yes sir. I'm fascinated by the theory."

"OK, Seems like you understand this crazy Donsaii math and, as you've run us through it, so far it does agree with existing physical evidence. However, let's assume that the 'faster than light' part of her theory is as ridiculous as it appears and that no one else in physics is taken in by it. Some theoretician is going to poke a hole in her math any day now. But, there might be, just might be, some people believing other parts of Donsaii's theory. Do you see any other testable phenomena that we can attack?"

Attack? Ell thought to herself. *That's pretty prejudicial.* "Sir, I've been thinking about the observer phenomenon in the double slit experiment where single photons act like waves if no observer determines which slit the photon goes through and like particles if there is an observer?"

"Yes, yes, we're physicists," he said impatiently, "we know *all* about the double slit experiment."

"Well, if Donsaii's theory is right, the methods so far used to observe the photon interfere with the connection of her cloud of photon manifestations through the postulated 5th dimension." Ell found it weird to be referring to herself in the third person.

"Come on Symonds! I suppose you think we should find a way to observe that doesn't interfere with that connection?"

"Um, yes sir."

"But I'll bet you don't have *any* ideas as to just how you are accomplish that little miracle?"

"Um, no sir."

He sighed disgustedly, "I was afraid of that. We need proposals that have some possibility that there's a mechanism that we can build to test them. Even if you don't know how to build a mechanism, you at least need to propose an observable physical phenomenon and then we can figure out whether it is feasible to construct a means to examine that phenomenon.

Ell said nothing and Johnson sighed again, "Do you understand how we might build something to test 'spin bumping'?"

"Uh yes sir. In broad terms anyway."

"OK, stay after the lab meeting and we'll talk specifics."

~~~

After the meeting Dr. Johnson brusquely took Ell through the lab, pointing out some of the equipment he thought might be useful in testing spin bumping, then suggested a whole list of equipment she could check out from the department's supply room. "You're going to need to read through the manuals and documentation on this equipment. Then find some published papers that used each piece of equipment so you can see how other investigators have used the instruments for similar studies in the past. Figure out how you might assemble something to test this 'spin bumping' crap. And, sure, spend some time thinking about how you could observe double slit photons without disturbing this ridiculous 5th dimension connection too. But, what you really want is a prediction that can be tested robustly enough that detractors won't be able to criticize our testing apparatus when Donsaii's predictions don't pan out."

"Yes sir." Ell said meekly.

"You may feel like I'm throwing you in the deep end here." Ell nodded. "But that's where great physicists are born, they learn to swim."

He turned abruptly and, as usual, left without saying goodbye, leaving Ell cross-eyed over the mixed metaphor. She snorted, *Born by learning to swim?*

~~~

Ell returned to her tiny apartment, cooked a frozen pizza and spent the night familiarizing herself with the online manuals for the equipment Dr. Johnson had suggested. The next day after running her first "Intro to physics" lab, she searched the literature for publications where other researchers had used the lab equipment she now had at her disposal. It turned out that reading those papers really did help her understand how the equipment could be used—though not necessarily how it could be used for her own experiment.

Over the next few days she began trying to set up an

apparatus to test spin bumping. As Professor Smythe had suggested, she intended to attempt it using entangled carbon 60 buckyballs in order to have a large symmetrical molecule which she could immobilize, then bump the spin on the shell electrons of one of the carbons according to the predictions of her new math.

~~~

Roger came over and watched her a moment. Her concentration appeared fierce, "Hey Ellen, what'cha doin'?"

"I'm trying to figure out how to immobilize a buckyball so that I can probe it with the atomic force microscope."

"Hmmm, aren't you just trying to perturb the electrons on a carbon molecule that's part of a symmetrical large carbon molecule?"

"Yes."

"Well, some atomic force microscopy probes already have a carbon nanotube attached to their tips. They use it as a "point" to make the probe 'sharper.' If it didn't matter to your project whether the AFM probe was poking the molecule, or the carbon macromolecule was on the AFM probe, you could just use a probe with a carbon macromolecule already on it."

"AFM tips really come that way?" She eyed him suspiciously, "Or are you just riding me?"

"Yep," he grinned, "they come that way. Hey, we lab rats are going out for beers tonight. And, I'm thinking you owe me a beer for telling you about the probes, eh?"

"Oh, I'm not old enough..." Ell suddenly remembered that her Ellen Symonds persona *was* old enough to drink, "I mean, 'young enough' to be fooled into buying you a drink. I think you probably owe *me* a beer for providing a new target for Johnson's wrath at the lab meetings, don't you?"

Roger laughed, "Tell you what, I'll buy you a beer for providing a target and you buy me a beer for the AFM suggestion. We're leaving at 6 and going to West 87. You up for it?"

Ell considered, it was a Friday night and it would be good to get out and make some friends. "Sure, if I'm not done here, I'll just meet you there a little later."

~~~

Ell felt a little weird walking past the bouncer whose AI undoubtedly queried her "Ellen" AI, "Fred," and got a purported age of 23. The bouncer hardly glanced at her, trusting the tech completely. This being her first time in a bar, she goggled as she looked around at all the huge screens showing various sporting events. There were people ranging from students to construction workers seated at tables and in booths. A number of actual hardware games such as pool and foosball tables were scattered around.

She walked up to Roger and poked him in the ribs, "Hey, nice wild goose chase you sent me on!"

"What do you mean?"

"Yeah, AFM probes *do* come with carbon nanotubes attached, but those nanotubes aren't entangled with another molecule! I'm embarrassed to admit I wasted an hour finding and ordering a probe before I considered *that* little detail!"

"Oops! I must tell you however, that that's the very first time I've ever made a mistake." He grinned unrepentantly down at her.

Ell glared at him, "This means that I *don't* owe you a

beer for the probe suggestion. You, however, still owe me a drink for catching all of Johnson's flack."

Roger's eyes widened, then Ell heard Johnson's voice over her shoulder, "Ms. Symonds, are you impugning my teaching methods by calling them 'flack'?"

Ell ducked her head and turned to see Johnson right behind her with a beer in his hand, "Uh, no sir!" She was relieved to see a twinkle in Johnson's eye.

"Good, because that's how great physicists are born, they learn to defend themselves."

"*Really* sir? How long have you been cultivating these mixed metaphors?"

To her relief he grinned again, "That's how great physicists grow, they plow under some metaphors. Roger's a poor grad student who can't possibly afford to buy you a beer, so I'm buying. What'll you have?"

"Uh, a Coke sir."

"You don't have to teetotal just because I'm here. I'd be happy to get you a beer."

Ell gulped, feeling guilty, but having decided that she didn't want to take advantage of her false identity to drink underage, she said, "It's OK, sir, I don't drink. A Coke'd be great though, thanks."

Johnson turned and left without saying anything. Ell turned back to Roger, "Is he mad that I didn't have a beer?"

"Nope. You worried because he didn't say anything, just went back to the bar?"

"Yeah, kinda."

"Get used to it. Haven't you noticed he never says good bye or in any way indicates the conclusion of a conversation?"

"Well, yeah."

"Just how he is. I'm pretty sure he's got Asperger's

syndrome."

"Huh?"

"You know. A kind of autism. Very high functioning but poor social skills. He's genius level physics, but weird to talk to. And as you're finding out, he can be *very* hard to get along with."

"Oh." Ell saw Johnson returning with her Coke, so she stopped talking to Roger and waved to the other grad students sitting around the little table. "How's it goin'?"

They all nodded and responded with some version of "fine." A redheaded young man Ell hadn't seen before said, "I'm Jerry, from the Sponchesi lab."

Roger said, "Sorry, I forgot you hadn't met everyone. This is Ellen Symonds. Dr. Johnson's assigned her to try to test that new theory of Donsaii's."

A chorus of "Ouch," and "Poor girl," came from the group.

Johnson stepped up and handed Ell her Coke. "What are you guys moaning about? It shouldn't take her long to prove *that* theory wrong. She's going to get an easy paper out of it."

Roger said, "Proving a negative is tough though."

Johnson rolled his eyes. "Please! That theory has so many holes in it; you could use it to strain spaghetti. With a little work she should be able to find all kinds of predictions that don't pan out!" In an abrupt change of topic, he said, "Anyone want to apply some real world physics to the pool table over there?"

Johnson, Roger, Jerry and another grad student named Al headed over to the nearest empty pool table, leaving Ell to sit with Emma, from the Sponchesi lab and James, a very handsome grad student, also from Johnson's lab. Emma said, "That's really tough, getting assigned that Donsaii paper. The math's *incomprehensible*."

Ell said, "I understand the math OK. I don't know much about testing apparati though."

Emma's brown eyes widened. "Really? Well if you can understand *that* math, I'll make you a deal. You help me with the math on my project, and I'll help you with your equipment."

James snorted, "Don't agree to that devil's bargain Ellen. The math on her project is really weird too! At least make her help you with your equipment first. Actually, that'd be a pretty good deal, Emma can make machines sing."

"Really?" Ell said, "I could sure use the help. What's your project?"

As Emma described her work James rolled his eyes and then looked around the room, bored with shop talk. Ell was relieved to learn that Emma's project involved a part of quantum theory that she was already familiar with because she'd worked with it some before coming up with her own theory. James interrupted, "How about some foosball? You ladies can gang up on me."

Emma shook her head, setting her tight brunette curls bouncing. "Just say no, Ellen. He's really good and loves to lord it over the rest of us."

James said, "How about if I just use one hand?"

Emma stared at him a moment, then stood with a sigh, "Come on Ellen, he won't rest until he's beaten us. You mind playing goalie?"

"I don't know. I haven't played much before." Ell said, nervous because she hadn't actually played foosball at all and didn't have any idea how well people normally performed at the game. She couldn't exhibit her actual hand-eye coordination for fear of freaking someone out. Nonetheless, she wanted to make friends and playing games seemed like it would be part of the package. She got up and walked with them over to a table.

Emma showed her the table and the two grips for the goalie player, advising "Ellen" that if she just positioned her players carefully and didn't move them much, she'd do OK.

James dropped a ball in and Emma started striking wildly at it with her forward players. However, the ball rolled past her to James' back row players. James quickly captured the ball and passed it up to his forward players where he stopped the ball and said, "Now Ellen, what you want to do is *try* to place your goalie players where they might stop my shot."

Ell didn't like his condescending tone, but wiggled her two rows of players around a little as if in response to his suggestion, placing them between his current location and the goal. She aggressively tamped down the excitement which was threatening to send her into her zone. "Like this?" she asked.

"Well yeah, but," James bumped the ball over to his middle player and hit it hard toward the opening in front of the goal that Ell'd left when she had positioned her players to block his side player.

Ell saw what he was doing and instinctively moved her player to block, moving much faster than she should have. Much faster than any normal person could react. So fast that her man was there in plenty of time to block the shot and drive it the length of the table into James' goal. In panicked realization of what she'd just done she wildly bounced her players back and forth, spinning them as if it had been an accidental flailing move rather than the purposeful shot it'd actually been.

Emma crowed delightedly and lifted her hand for a high five. "Oh yeah! Way to go. We should just go sit down while James is digesting *that* crow!"

Ell slapped her hand against Emma's saying, "I'm pretty lucky sometimes." She watched James' stunned expression out of the corner of her eye. They played more, Ell now careful to let most of James' shots sail right past her. She blocked a few, but barely.

No more driving them back to the other end!

~~~

Ell found herself back at the booth. As per his normal behavior, Johnson'd just walked out the door and gone home without saying goodbye to anyone. Emma and the handsome James seemed to be making eyes at each other and Ell was sitting between Roger and Jerry. Jerry had a great sense of humor and kept both of them in stitches with his analysis of the denizens of the bar, each of whom he proposed had an alter ego. "What about James?" Ell whispered. "What's his alter ego?"

"Oh him!" Jerry waved his hand deprecatingly, "He's actually a male escort for one of the services in town. Women needing a discreet man to accompany them to an old enemy's wedding and such; he's there to provide a little arm candy."

Ell snorted with mirth as she looked over at James' aquiline, blond good looks. "And Emma?"

"My goodness, you didn't know?" He leaned forward conspiratorially, "An industrial spy. No one's sure yet just what country she's spying for, but be very careful what you tell her about your discoveries on the infamous Donsaii project." Jerry and Roger both chortled delightedly at the mere thought of an industrial spy wanting any part of Ellen's project.

Ell lowered an eyebrow, "I'll be sure to freeze her out on the critical details." she said with a crooked grin. "What about Roger here? What's his alter ego?"

"Oh, that's just so sad. What you see here's all you get. Nothing more to ol' Rog' than what you already know. Shallow as a sheet of graphene is our Roger." Jerry grinned at Roger.

Roger snorted. "Not true! I've just completely concealed my alter ego behind this simple Clark Kent façade," he said, waving fingers past his face and upper body. He turned to Ell and stage whispered, "It's just that Jerry *cannot* envision my true depths!"

"OK, how about you Jerry? What's your alter ego?"

"Me? Li'l ol' me?" Jerry put his hand dramatically on his chest. He leaned forward and stage whispered, "Actually, I'm an *alien*, visiting from Alpha Centauri. I'm evaluating the human race for admission to the Galactic Congress. Unfortunately, I'm having to report that these beings I find myself surrounded with haven't even discovered the fifth dimension that connects quantum particles." He waggled his eyebrows at Ell, "You, my dear, are these meager humans only hope!"

"Well, I'd better get home and get my rest then. I'll need my strength to save our human race from you awful Centaurians!"

"Nooo!" the two young men said together. "The night is still young."

Ell, however, got up, checked with Allan to be sure her tab was paid and made for the door. She didn't want to be walking home after midnight, even if her little apartment was only six blocks away. She waved good bye to the group, but Jerry got up too, "Let me walk you home," he called.

"Walk home with an alien?" Ell eyed him suspiciously, "You wouldn't suck my brains out would you?"

"Of course not! Not on our first walk home! I have to lull your suspicions with insincere niceties for a while first."

~~~

As they left Roger eyed them pensively. With that nose she might not be very cute, but there was something about Ellen he liked. He'd always liked smart women, and the way she calmly took Johnson's brutal questioning, answering questions about the Donsaii math so unhesitatingly... it really impressed him. *She's someone I'd like to spend time with,* he thought to himself. He sighed, *if only I didn't get so tongue tied around women.*

~~~

As Ell and Jerry walked the streets to her place with the heat of the day gone, the evening was pleasant if a little muggy. Jerry kept up a witty banter that cheered Ell. Seeing a few winos in the alleys, Ell realized that her new neighborhood really wasn't that great a place for a young woman to be out alone at night. It made her truly appreciate his gesture in walking her home.

When they arrived at her building, Ell suddenly worried that Jerry might expect to be invited up to her apartment? She realized that if she did invite him up, he'd encounter items that gave away her disguise. At the main door she turned to him saying, "My suspicions have been lulled. I'm still concerned that you just want to suck out my brains, nonetheless I appreciate your protection from all the Rigellians living in the alleys between here and West 87."

Jerry frowned, "Rigellians?"

"The ones disguised as winos?"

"Ah, you can see through their masquerades! Bravo."

For a second Jerry leaned closer as if for a kiss, but then to Ell's relief, he said, "Hey, no problem. See you on Monday," he winked, "*if* I successfully avoid the Rigellians on my walk home." He gave an exaggerated shiver, then turned and headed back down the street. Ell thumped upstairs and gratefully took off her "fat pants," as she thought of the silicone padding that enlarged her butt. Then she carefully rearranged her closet so that her spare fat pants, silicone nose prostheses, dark hair mousse and skin bronzers were hidden away from any but the most determined prying eyes.

In case I have a guest sometime, she thought.

In bed, while she tried to think about her testing apparatus, she found herself wondering what was wrong with her that Jerry *didn't* ask to come up. Then she chastised herself for worrying *because* he'd acted like a gentleman. Then, with some embarrassment at herself, she pondered how she hadn't thought that her appearance mattered—*until* she found the opposite sex's eyes were no longer magnetically drawn to her.

***

On Monday Ell asked Emma for help setting up her apparatus and found that the young woman really did have a knack for electronic equipment. They made a good team because Ell had the manuals for the equipment mostly committed to memory and Emma could explain to Ell what the manufacturer meant by some of the obscure directions Ell'd read. After her late morning class, Ell spent a couple of hours helping Emma better understand the math for Emma's own project.

That afternoon at the 3 PM research meeting Johnson was in a real mood. He jumped on everyone about their progress on their projects. Eventually he turned to Ell, "Symonds, have you made any progress on finding more easily testable predictions from that mess of a paper Donsaii wrote?"

"No sir. But I've made progress on setting up an apparatus for testing the spin bumping prediction."

"Oh, that crap!" Johnson rubbed at his scalp, "And have you figured out how you're going to deal with the criticisms that are inevitably going to be directed at your apparatus when it doesn't work and you claim *that* disproves the hypothesis?"

In a quiet voice, "No sir."

He threw up his hands and said, "*Don't* waste much more time on that spin bumping crap. I want you spending most of your time on developing other testable predictions from that gobbledygook." He turned and began badgering James about his project.

When the meeting broke up Johnson peremptorily said, "Ellen, take me to see your setup."

Ell's equipment was set up on a large lab table. Johnson rolled his eyes as soon as he saw the table, pointing out that she needed some form of vibration isolation. He then went on to angrily criticize each section of her apparatus. Ell felt ignorant and ashamed well before he was done.

After Johnson left Ell sat and stared at her

equipment, thinking that she couldn't possibly figure out how to do this right. Roger came over and put his hand on her shoulder. "Hey, you probably feel pretty dumb right now, huh?"

"Yeah!" Ell said with a disgusted sigh.

"Well, he *is* an ass, but hey, take comfort in the fact that the crap he just rained on you was nothing compared to his first evaluation of *my* setup. Cheer up, that's about as good as it gets when you're working in the Johnson lab."

"'That's as good as it gets,' is supposed to cheer me up?"

Roger grinned, "Yup, that's as good as I get at cheering you up too."

"Crap! Is it possible to transfer to another professor?"

"Hah! Sure, if you can find one who'll take you, but you'll lose ground."

"Well, thanks for *trying* to cheer me up, yet somehow leaving me even more depressed."

Roger wandered back over to his setup and Ell sat, chin in her hands, staring at her setup. The more she looked at it the more she began to realize that, despite Johnson's brutal assessment of her current setup, his suggestions were on target. If she did change the things he'd blasted her, the setup really would be a lot better. If only he could teach her without belittling her in the process. She squared her shoulders, gritted her teeth and headed off to the equipment room to get more supplies.

Chapter Five

Weeks had passed while Ell worked on setting up her apparatus. Chief Bowers called to tell her that the prosecution of her kidnappers had fallen into a morass of legal manipulations and diplomatic negotiations. In Bowers' mind there was no longer any doubt that China itself was involved, not just protecting their citizens who'd gotten in trouble. Bowers warned Ell to remain alert because he felt the organization that the kidnappers were a part of remained active. He thought they were probably searching for her but having trouble due to her disguise.

She'd become comfortable teaching her beginning physics lab and found it a lot of fun. Her own classes were a mixture of things she already knew and a few interesting things that made her glad she'd attended the class. The classes didn't waste much of her time because she'd become adept at *pretending* to listen to stuff she already knew, while mentally working on her own theory. Friday nights at West 87 had become a comfortable routine and pretty much Ell's only social life. A lot of the physics grad students went there regularly and she'd met almost all of the other grads there on one night or another.

But today was the day when her theory met its big test. The apparatus was set up and all the different parts had been thoroughly tested and calibrated. She'd given up on buckyballs because it was difficult to position two buckyballs identically. Now she was using laser cooled gaseous condensates. She had them entangled and was ready to spin bump the first one and see if she could detect the bump at the second entanglement. Taking a deep breath she activated her bumper while keeping her eye on the display of the detector.

Nothing happened! She keyed the bumper again, still nothing. She pounded the key…

Ell's shoulders slumped. She'd *told* herself it would be a miracle if it worked the first time she tried it, but she'd been *so* sure…

Roger's voice came over her shoulder, "Somebody shoot your dog?"

"No," Ell was dismayed to hear a quaking in her voice. She cleared her throat. "It just didn't work, is all…" Her voice trailed off.

"Oh, crap. How many times have you tried it so far?"

"Um, this is the first time."

"What! And you're depressed? No! No! No! Consider yourself very, very lucky! If your experiment *had* worked the first time you tried it, the rest of us would have to take you to the woodshed."

"The woodshed?"

"For a beating! *No one's* experiment *ever* works the first time, if yours had, our jealousy would have demanded we give you a most severe pounding!"

"Oh." Ell felt cheered somewhat. "So the laws of physics were against me?"

"Yup. Murphy's infamous law in full force."

"So, it'll work the second time?" She grinned crookedly back at him.

"Hah! The optimism of you young people astonishes

me!" He put his hand on his chest and leaned back as if looking down on her from years of wisdom. "I'll buy you a beer at West 87 to assuage your pain."

"But it's Thursday."

"*Tomorrow* night, we'll help you drink your pain away."

"But I don't drink."

"Amend that. *We'll* drink your pain away."

That afternoon Johnson quizzed Ell about her project as usual. His eyebrows went up in mock surprise, "It didn't work! Really?"

"No sir." Ell responded in a small voice.

"Of *course* it didn't work! The question is; can you prove it wasn't because of a failure of your apparatus? Do you have evidence that you successfully spin bumped the proximate condensate?"

"Uh, no sir."

"Well for *God's sake*, Symonds! You have to show you actually bumped the near condensate before anyone is going to worry about whether it might have transmitted the bump to the entangled condensate!"

"Yes sir."

"How are you going to determine that?"

After a pause Ell said, "I guess I could move my detector over and set it up on the near condensate to be sure I can actually detect bumping there?"

"Well, of course! I can't believe you tried to do the final experiment without first making sure of the spin bumping crap!"

"No sir. I mean, yes sir. I'll get right on it."

"OK, however, remember I've told you I don't want you wasting much more time on this spin bumping crap. You need to move on to something with a *chance* it might pan out and *pronto*." He turned to the next grad student at the table.

~~~

Ell felt like an idiot for not considering such a basic step and was working hard on resetting the detector when Johnson came by to look at her setup before leaving for the day. He made some suggestions which were helpful in the extreme, but again left her feeling stupid for not recognizing the problems he'd seen so quickly.

Of course, the fact that he pointed the issues out as if he was speaking to an imbecile probably contributed to her feelings of inadequacy.

As Johnson was leaving, he turned back to her and rode the same old saw, "You've really got to get cracking on other testable predictions in that Donsaii theory. I'm almost positive you're not going to be able to convincingly prove this spin bumping crap's wrong. You're going to have to attack her theory from a different angle to get a reasonable paper out of this. Think, woman! Think!"

He walked on out the door... as usual without saying goodbye.

Roger came over and patted her on the shoulder, "You really should have a beer with us tomorrow night." He walked on over to the coffee machine and filled his cup.

~~~

Friday came and went without much progress. Emma helped Ell reset and calibrate her detector, but it failed to detect 'bumping' at the near condensate which left Ell with the frustrating puzzle of whether the 'bumper' didn't work, whether the detector didn't work, or whether the bumping she'd predicted wasn't actually physically possible?

~~~

James sat down next to Ellen at West 87. She appeared to be moping over her Coke. "Why you down in the dumps cute stuff?"

"'Cute stuff?'" She said looking up at him. "Didn't that kind of slang go out about five decades ago?"

James put his hands up, "Just tryin' to cheer a girl up! Don't shoot the messenger."

"Besides, aren't you and Emma an item?"

James' eyebrows rose, "No way!" He leaned closer and said in a stage whisper, "She's *much* too good for me."

Ellen leaned back and looked him over, "Well, *that's* certainly true. But," she arched her eyebrows, "I assume you're saying then, that I might be down at your level?"

James put his hands up again, "Damn! Women! Twisting everything I say! Let's go back to, 'Why you down in the dumps, Ellen?'"

~~~

To himself James thought that if Ellen didn't wear so much makeup she might be cute. He wondered if she thought the makeup made her beaky nose less noticeable? *And of course then there's also the matter of her huge butt. Taking off the makeup wouldn't help that. Still, I like her, looks or no.*

"Arggh," Ellen said, "I haven't been having any luck with my experimental setup. Nothing I'm doing's working at all!"

"Welcome to science! If it was easy, *everybody'd* be doin' it."

"Yeah, yeah, yeah. So I hear. I didn't think it was supposed to be *this* hard though. At least something I'm doing should be working correctly shouldn't it?"

"Nah, consider Murphy! Let me buy you a beer and we'll toast him!"

"I don't drink, and I've already got a Coke. But thanks."

"OK, how about I teach you the finer points of pool. A simple game, based on physics. It doesn't go like you plan either."

"Sure." Ellen said, getting up, "It'll take my mind off my misery. You'll have to teach me how to play though."

~~~

They rented a table and James showed her how to pick out a straight cue and rack the balls. After he broke the balls, he took time to explain how the object ball was driven directly away from the point where the cue ball made contact with it.

Ell realized that it really was a game based on ordinary mechanical physics and she soon became very interested in those mechanics, successfully forgetting about her lab failures. With her phenomenal hand eye coordination, after a few shots she could control the object ball's direction exactly and was forced to begin missing pockets on purpose so that James wouldn't be disturbed by how well she played. She noticed that he hit the cue ball low sometimes, putting backspin on it in an effort to control where the cue ball would wind up for his next shot. She experimented with applying spin until she could place the cue ball pretty much where she wanted, though she purposefully didn't place it in advantageous locations, again for fear of appearing to be unreasonably good.

James, being a moderately good player, was nonetheless astonished by her play. She claimed it was her first game yet she had nearly as many balls in as he did. "Are you sure you've never played before?"

"Well, a few games." Ell swore to herself, realizing that, despite making many intentional mistakes, she must still be playing better than most beginners did. She let her pool cue strike the cue ball off center with a rattle that sent the cue ball into a corner pocket.

A gruff voice sounded over Ell's shoulder with a wash of beer breath, "Hey, pretty boy. All the tables are full so we're challenging you for this one. Well, challenging you if you can beat Girly here? Otherwise we'll have to challenge *her*!" He guffawed at his wit.

Ell looked back. A large, grizzly man in jeans, boots and a stained t-shirt stood there, screwing a pool cue together. He seemed out of place in this bar that mostly catered to students from the university, but she'd seen working men and occasional biker types in the bar before. She looked at James. He had a pinched look on his face as if the challenge upset him. Wondering if she could defuse the situation she asked, "Maybe you and your partner could challenge the two of us to a game of doubles?"

The man sniggered. "Sure!" he rumbled.

James missed his next two shots, so Ell did too. The man pounded his cue on the floor, "Geez, Pretty Boy, you too scared to make a shot?"

Ell glared at the man, "Take it easy, everyone has a bad run now and then." The man laughed and went to the bar to order another beer. Ell made one shot and then missed the next. She and James both had one ball on the table now, with the eight ball waiting. But, with her miss, Ell'd carefully placed the cue ball with a good line on James' last ball. James took a deep breath, shook his shoulders out, carefully didn't look at the two biker types and sunk his last ball, then the eight. Ell turned to the bikers and said, "Hi, I'm Ellen and this is James."

"Bill," the man said, then jerked his thumb at his even larger friend who wore a leather vest over his t-shirt, "that's 'Silent Joe,' but most of us just call him Silent." Silent stood, took the rack and started racking the balls without saying a word.

James said, "Ell, let's just let them have the table…"

Bill guffawed, "Naw, that wouldn't be right. Just *scarin'* you two away. We'd rather win it."

James grimaced, obviously feeling insulted, but shrugged his shoulders at Ell.

For her part Ell found herself irritated. She jerked her chin at James and said, "Go ahead and break."

James' break was creditable and the nine ball went in, but he missed the easy followup shot.

Bill proceeded to put in five balls, barely missing the sixth, heckling James and Ell on each one, "See, *that's* how it's done pretty boy… Now, what you do is line up your shots and *stroke* them in… You' gotta have *balls* to play this game though… *Real* men don' miss shots like this…" Ell thought to herself that it could've been pleasant ribbing, like guys often engaged in during games—but it wasn't. There was a mean edge to it and the emphasis on certain words lent an insulting sexual connotation to them.

Ell was furious by the time Bill missed a shot, so she paused for a moment to contemplate the table and get her feelings back in control, determined to just miss her shot and let them have the table. She was sorry she hadn't just let them have it when James suggested it. But, Bill mistook her hesitation. "Come on Girly, just go ahead and miss your shot so's we can get this over with." He grinned.

Ell looked at him a moment, "It's Ell..." she cleared her throat, "Ellen... Not 'Girly.'"

He guffawed and slapped his knee, then elbowed Silent. "Oops, my mistake."

Ell stared at him a moment longer, her right eyelid twitched a couple of times like it often did when she was irritated. Then she ran the table.

After she drilled the eight ball into the corner pocket, she looked up at Bill and Silent who looked on a little goggle eyed. "We'll keep the table ourselves, thanks." She picked up the rack and started racking the balls. She looked up at James who was quite goggle eyed himself and winked at him.

James said, "I thought you'd only played a 'few games?'"

Ell grinned up at him and shrugged, "Maybe *quite* a few."

James broke again and they resumed play, Ell playing just a little better than James now. With the sullen bikers still standing behind her, Ell suddenly felt anxious to get the game done and go back to sit down. She noted out of the corner of her eye that several more grinning biker types had walked over and were ribbing Bill and Silent.

Ell pocketed the eight ball with an easy shot and picked up the tray for the balls so they could return them. Bill stepped up to the table and snarled, "Hundred bucks says you can't do that again."

"What, make the eight ball in the corner pocket there?"

"No! You know what I mean. Play us again and win."

"Oh! You're absolutely right." Ell put her hands up in surrender. "I just got lucky. You guys can have the table." She said this pleasantly, smiling at him as unthreateningly as possible. Inside she cursed herself for running the table earlier.

"Hundred bucks!" he grated out.

Cheerfully, "Oh! No thanks. I don't gamble." She carefully didn't look at James to see how he was taking this.

"You'll play us, or I'll bust up your pretty little boy toy," he said, jerking his head at James.

Now Ell did look at James. White faced, he licked his lips nervously. "No, no, this was all just a misunderstanding." Ell said, "I just got really lucky. You can have the table. It's all good." She picked up her pool cue and began twisting it in her hands as if she were nervous.

Bill jerked his chin up at James who was about twelve feet away. "Pretty Boy, let's you and me go outside." he snarled.

James backed up a step, but Silent had been standing behind him and James bumped into the massive man. Bill stepped toward James. Ell, feeling herself dropping into the zone, took a couple of quick steps beside him and reached to grab his elbow. Bill shrugged her off and said, "Pretty boy, outside! Or do I have to mess you up in here?"

Ell, consciously slowing her voice so it would sound normal, said, "If you really want to play..."

"Naw, now I got my heart set on beatin' the crap outta your pretty boyfriend."

Bill lunged toward James.

Ell slipped her pool cue between Bill's legs and started screaming hysterically.

Bill crashed to the floor and skidded into Silent Joe's feet, James having reflexively stepped to the side.

Ell, keeping a grip on the pool cue and still yelling, swiveled her head to make sure the bouncers were on their way over.

Silent saw the bouncers coming and grabbed at Bill as he came up off the floor fighting mad. Bill shook off Silent's hand and turned back toward Ell, throwing a massive roundhouse punch. Ell dodged just underneath the punch while snapping her head back as if she'd actually been hit.

She pretended to stumble backward against the pool table.

Recovering, Bill took another mighty swing, this time Ell dodged her head out of the way, but let his fist strike the handle of the pool cue she'd held next to her head. This strike was solid enough to split Bill's knuckle and make a loud cracking sound. At the "crack" Ell flung herself backward across the table like the blow had struck.

The bouncers arrived, immobilized Bill and summoned the police.

AI's were interrogated for their audio-video record of the events and Bill arrested for assault and battery. Thankfully no one examined Ell for bruises. Instead, they trusted the video evidence which convincingly made it appear that, with no more serious provocation than winning a pool game, she'd been struck hard twice. Roger, Emma, Al and Jerry had rushed over to be sure James and Ell were OK, but eventually wandered back over to their table during the police interrogations.

When the police released James and Ell, they walked over to join the others at their usual booth. Emma looked up as they approached and said, "What the heck happened?! We saw you guys playing pool with those biker guys and thought it was kind of weird, but no one noticed anything else until Symonds started screaming! You can really make some noise girl!"

James looked down, then back up at the group. "Uh, we were just playing each other when they challenged us to a game for the table."

Ell said, "James had the common sense to tell them they could just have the table but I was an idiot and told them we'd play them for it." She turned to James, "Sorry, I should have followed your lead."

James winced, "Yeah... I've been around guys like that before. They can be real assholes. But, maybe if I'd stood up to them it would have defused the situation."

"No!" Ell exclaimed, "I don't think there's *any* defusing guys like that. You were really smart to just tell them they could have the table. I think that Bill guy wanted to start a fight from the beginning!"

James shrugged his shoulders unhappily, "Yeah, maybe so."

Emma said, "But what happened? Did he punch you James?"

"Naw, he was coming after me but he fell down. Did you trip him with your pool cue Ellen?"

Ell tried to look sheepish, "Maybe? It felt like his foot hit my cue."

James spoke to his AI, "Let's see the video of the attack." James' AI forwarded it to the group and they all watched in slow motion on their HUDs as Bill leaned forward and stepped out with his left foot. As soon as he started moving Ell's pool cue swung out in front of his right leg and behind his left so that when Bill's right foot moved to follow the left, he tripped over the pool cue, falling violently outstretched onto the floor. The video was disturbed by James' quick step to the right as he avoided Bill, but Ell felt fairly sure they'd accept that she'd *accidentally* tripped the man. At least she hoped everyone thought she had at most made a reflexive move with the pool cue rather than recognizing that she had carefully planned out exactly what she was going to do and perfectly executed it with her zone enhanced reflexes.

With relief Ell heard Roger say, "Wow, Ellen. That stab with the pool cue couldn't have been more perfect if you'd planned it that way."

They all watched the video as Bill scrambled back up from the floor, rage on his face and made his roundhouse swing at Ell. As her head snapped back in the video, Ell was pleased to see that it really did look like Bill'd connected. She heard her friends uttering versions of "Ouch!" or "Damn!" When Bill made his second swing and Ell leaped back across the table, she herself easily recognized her own muscles contracting to throw herself backward as well as positioning the pool cue so it took the blow instead of her head.

But no one else seemed to notice.

Emma said, "Ellen, we should take you to the hospital. You might have a serious head injury after getting hit like that." Emma reached for Ell's face to look for swelling or bruises. Ell shrank away, worried that Emma might disturb her makeup or her nose prosthesis. "No! No, I'm fine. Really! His first swing just grazed me and the second one mostly hit my pool cue. I'm not hurt, at most I might have a bruise tomorrow."

Emma said, "Well, at the least you should stay at my

place tonight in case you have a concussion or something like that."

Relieved, Ell said, "I can do that. But no hospitals! I *can't* afford a hospital when I feel fine."

The group chattered excitedly about the fight for a while longer and then the conversation gradually turned to other things. James leaned over to Ell and whispered, "Hey, let's keep your pool skills a secret for now. I'd really like to surprise the Professor with them sometime."

"Uh, OK. But I really did get lucky. I don't normally run the table."

"Yeah, sure. And I'm as retarded as Biker Billy. You may not run the table every time, but you're really, really good at pool. I can't believe how you sandbagged me with that, 'I've never played before' line and I bought it." James chuckled, "It's embarrassing to remember how I was trying to teach you the basics."

"OK," Ell said turning back to listen to Al.

Al had started telling the group about a lecture he'd attended on exoplanets. "So they've turned the Large Radiotelescope Array to look at over eighty percent of the known planets that are in the liquid water zone. None of them are transmitting. Nada, zilch, zip. No radio transmissions at all. We're talking thousands of planets that should or could be life bearing. I just can't believe that *none* of them have developed intelligent life."

"Intelligence might be a lot rarer than we'd expect."

"Do we know if they have life at all, much less intelligent life?"

Al said, "I think he said that over fifty percent have oxygen atmospheres. The assumption is that, because oxygen's so reactive, an oxygen atmosphere means life.

Something has to be constantly producing more O2 or it'd all get bound up. Of course they can't be sure."

Jerry said, "They might be intelligent without using radio." Ell felt goose bumps run down her spine. Jerry continued, "Humans have been intelligent for tens of thousands of years but have only had radio for a little over a hundred."

Ell continued to have chills. She'd thought that Jerry meant intelligent beings might communicate with something *other* than radio, whereas he'd just meant that they might not have *discovered* radio. However, it suddenly seemed blindingly obvious to her.

Maybe this could explain Fermi's paradox regarding the vast number of stars which should have developed intelligent life and the question of "where are they?" In other words, since there should be thousands of other intelligent species in the galaxy we *should* be able to pick up their radio messages with SETI.

But, not if they didn't use radio! Of course! The reason the human race hadn't detected advanced civilizations communicating by radio is that advanced civilizations communicated with something better. Certainly, over interstellar distances radio was far too slow to be useful! Advanced civilizations would *have* to use something faster. Could they be using something like Ell's spin bumping or other instantaneous communication methods with a connection through her postulated fifth dimension? Ell, mind working furiously on this, completely missed the next minutes of conversation, eyes focused on her glass of Coke.

Emma shoved her again, "Hey, Ellen, you OK?"

Ell looked up and turned, still glassy eyed, "Huh?"

"Huh, yourself. I was beginning to think concussion had set in. You ready to head home?"

Ell puzzled over this a moment. *Why was Emma asking that?* Then she remembered that she was supposed to go home with Emma for observation, just in case she actually had a concussion. "Uh, sure." She finished her Coke, "Let's go."

Jerry stood, "I'll walk you."

Emma turned and curtsied minutely, "Thank you kind sir."

Jerry grinned sketching a tiny bow with waving hand in return, "Ah, it is but the least I can do."

When they stepped outside, a large shadow separated itself from the wall, Ell turned quickly to see Silent Joe gazing at them. Jerry blanched. Ell stared at Silent and began to drop into the zone but the huge man merely inclined his head. "Nice shootin'," he said gruffly. "Bill was acting like a jerk. Got what he deserved." Then he leaned his bulk back up against the wall.

Jerry, Emma and Ell made to pass, all staying a little to the far side of the sidewalk. Allan whispered in Ell's earpiece. "Silent Joe's real name is Joseph Cylend. He's forwarded his contact information with a note to reach out to him if you ever need help."

"That's... astonishing," Ell subvocalized. "Tell him thanks."

When they reached Emma's apartment Ell began to worry about hiding her "fat pants." As she had feared, Emma apparently intended for Ell to sleep on Emma's queen sized bed with her. Ell successfully avoided this by lying down on the couch, pulling a large knitted throw over herself and then quickly feigning sleep. When Emma tried to get her to come to bed, she grumbled and snuffled and demanded to be left alone where she was.

As promised, Emma woke her up once in the middle of the night to be sure she was OK and not suffering from a serious head injury.

Ell had to pretend to be muzzy with sleep when she'd actually been lying awake, her mind racing over the possibilities of interstellar communications through the postulated 5th dimension. She felt like there was something about the possibility of interstellar communication that should clue her in on the way she did her experiments. But that clue hovered just out of reach—like a word on the "tip of your tongue" that you can't quite remember.

Laurence E Dahners

Chapter Six

Weeks followed with little progress. It took several weeks just to tweak her setup so Ell could successfully detect bumping at the location where it was actually being performed. Then more weeks were required to successfully entangle condensates and confirm they were entangled.

Then more weeks passed trying to detect evidence of the first condensate's bumping at the second condensate. Those attempts were all without success.

Ell hadn't really experienced a major failure at something she'd focused on in the past. Well, except for physical tasks requiring endurance.

She and Emma'd started running together for exercise. This was at Emma's suggestion. Ell suspected that Emma was hoping some work would get Ell's butt down to a smaller size. She liked getting exercise but, as usual, her limited endurance made it agonizing trying to keep up with Emma on their morning runs. Hauling the silicone fat pants around with her made it even worse.

The running and the frustration she experienced with failure after failure of her bumping setup made her lose weight. She slept even less than her usual three to four hours per night. Her hair got brittle, perhaps made worse by Ell's need to constantly apply the dark mousse to cover her reddish blond hair. At least the mousse covered the broken ends.

She felt a hand on her shoulder and lifted her head from her desk. She looked around blearily and found

Roger standing at her shoulder, "Hey."

Roger looked concerned. He said. "Ell, you OK?"

"Yeah, sure, what's up?"

"Our three PM meeting is in a couple of minutes. I've been worried about you though. You don't look so good."

"Yeah, this experiment is crushing me. Nothing seems to work and I've started having nightmares about it."

Roger's brow knotted as he looked at her with concern. He'd really started to like the odd looking young woman over the past couple of months. He found her ability to handle the math in Donsaii's paper astonishing. Her equanimity in so far handling the incredible frustrations of her experiment was inspiring. Seeing the project getting the best of her made him feel sad.

Ell got up and they went down the hall to the lab meeting. When they got there Dr. Johnson was in a terrible mood, ripping each of the grad students as they reported what was happening with their particular projects. But when he got to Ell's project it got even worse. "Do you mean to tell me that you're *still* working on that spin bumping crap? How many times do I have to tell you to move on to the double slit aspects of Donsaii's paper? I want you to disassemble that spin bumping setup tomorrow! *Stop* wasting time!"

Roger felt aghast. Ellen had looked so down before they came to the meeting, he was afraid this tongue lashing would be the straw that broke the camel's back. Her eyes dropped down to the table a moment, and she looked up with a drawn face. "If I promised to only work on spin bumping on my own time, say evenings and weekends, could I leave it set up?"

Laurence E Dahners

Johnson's eyebrows shot up, "You'd be thinking about it all the time. Nothing'd get done during regular hours!"

Ell's expression remained dull and flat as she said, "I'm sorry, spin bumping is what I *want* to work on. If I can't work on that here, I'll find a different graduate program to work in."

Roger was astonished to hear Ellen giving Johnson an ultimatum when he was in this current mood, but even more astonished when Johnson leaned back in his chair. He looked up at the ceiling a moment then sighed. "OK, I'm sure you guys are all aware that physicists under thirty make most of the really big discoveries because they try *stupid* stuff that older physicists *know* won't work. *But*... you need to consider that thousands of foolish attempts at crap that older physicists know won't work, *don't* actually work. Though I'm 'old' I am *not* an idiot." He settled his chair back into place and stared at Ellen, "However, I *won't* stifle you Symonds. If you want to work nights and weekends on something that's a complete waste of time, go ahead. However, don't expect *any* help from me while you tilt at your windmill. That project is now yours and *yours alone*, to fail with, or even against all reasonable possibility, to succeed."

The grad students looked at each other with raised eyebrows, stunned to hear Johnson the tyrant speaking as if they had choices? Then he leaned forward in his chair, "Now, tell me, what are your plans to look into the double slit phenomenon?"

Still in a flat and listless voice Ellen said, "OK, we can't try to detect which slit the photon passes with polarization or the like because such methods will break the fifth dimensional connection, so I've been looking for other means to register the passage of a photon. But there are two issues. First, that a method for detecting passage of a photon without stopping or deflecting the photon, and without breaking a fifth dimensional connection does not exist. Second, if Donsaii's correct, a single photon, if unobserved, would, in fact, be detected at both slits, but I'm not sure how we would prove that two photons had not been emitted?"

To his surprise Roger heard his own voice saying, "What if you used very high energy photons and detected them with flux sens..."

Ellen's eyebrows shot up. With an excited exclamation of "Yes!" she proceeded to detail a possible method, using the new flux sensors, much more fully fleshed out than the fuzzy idea Roger'd just had. Roger could hardly believe that she'd just heard his suggestion a moment ago.

Johnson, leaned back a moment with his lips pursed, then without saying anything he appeared somewhat mollified. He nodded, "When you publish that, some will still argue that you haven't completely disproved Donsaii, but it'll be a nail in the coffin." He turned to his next target.

***

Weeks passed with Ell working weekdays on the double slit experiment, then evenings and weekends on her entangled particles. She'd given up on the condensates and moved on to other particles and was back to carbon macromolecules. This particular Friday after work she entangled some long carbon nanotubes and was stimulating the near one with various means, not just spin bumping. She was heating the nanotube with a laser while varying a magnetic field around it when the laser developed an intermittent fault. Ell swore and slammed her fist on the counter, then unplugged the laser; she couldn't replace it now, the supply room was closed. She started shutting down her equipment. It was as she reached for the switch on the detector module that she noted the spikes on its screen. Ice flooded her veins as she slowly reached out and began turning the apparatus back on. It took another hour to reestablish the magnetic field at the strength it had been before. Then more minutes to reset the laser at the correct frequency. With the sensation that her hair was standing on end, she recognized that the laser emission wavelength was a multiple of the length of the nanotube. Then spikes showed up again on the detector, replicating the intermittent faults of the laser, though they were much larger than spin bumping should produce. They continued to appear after she picked up the detector and moved it into the other room. When she broke the circuit to the laser it caused the same spikes on the detector. Slowly she turned everything off and wandered dazedly out of the lab. She walked slowly to West 87, pondering what she had just witnessed and contemplating how it fit into her theory? She knew serendipity had played an enormous role in some of the most important scientific breakthroughs in the world— had she just witnessed a massively serendipitous event?

As she entered the bar, it suddenly came together for her. The laser wasn't causing the spin bumping she'd been working on... rather the resonance between the nanotube and the laser was activating the "photon-gluon resonance" phenomenon, also predicted by her math!

When it came to her, Ell'd stopped where she was and closed her eyes trying to visualize it in her mind. A bouncer grasped her elbow and gently moved her out of the flow of traffic. After a bit she opened her eyes and, looking up at her AI's displays on her HUD, she started having Allan run simulations of what she thought was happening.

~~~

Dr. Johnson had chosen this evening to go to West 87 with the grads as he did occasionally. Over at their regular booth, he turned irritably to Roger and asked, "What's gotten into Symonds now?"

When Johnson nodded her way, Roger noticed Ellen for the first time. He watched her standing immobile, apparently watching her AI monitors for a minute. He said, "I don't know, I'll go check on her."

When Roger got to her, Ell didn't notice him until he tapped her shoulder, "Ell?"

"Huh? Oh, hi Roger. I'll be over in a minute."

In fact it was more like fifteen minutes before she shook herself and walked over and sat down, still with a dazed look on her face. Her mind continued to jump from implication to implication of what had happened and to consider experiments she could do when she could check out more equipment.

Johnson said, "What's with you Symonds?"

"Uh, I just got a weird result out of the spin bumping apparatus that has me rethinking the whole..."

Johnson interrupted, "Oh Goddammit! Not more of that crap! You still haven't given that up?"

Startled by the vehemence of his reaction Ell said,

"Uhhh…"

Johnson interrupted again, "No, no, don't tell me, I can see you're going to keep wasting time on spin bumping until Hell won't have it. As long as you're making progress on the double slit experiment, I'll pretend I don't care." His tone abruptly shifted to pleasant, "Anybody up for a game of pool?"

Ell leaned back in her chair but James and Roger signaled assent. As they got up, James said, "Ellen, we need a fourth. Be my partner?"

Ell had been glaring at Johnson's back. She shook her head "no." She *didn't* want to hang out with the professor.

James leaned back to her and said, "Oh come on. It'll give you a chance to put the old man in his place. Don't you want a chance to get even for all those drubbings he gives you at the lab meetings?"

Ell tilted her head and looked at James speculatively. She narrowed her eyes, "OK."

Roger'd almost finished racking the balls and Johnson was chalking his cue when James and Ell arrived. Johnson looked up at them, mood shifted to nice, like his moods so often abruptly shifted, "So Symonds, you going to watch some physics in action?"

James said, "Oh no, she's going to play as my partner and we're going to win some beers from you two."

Roger looked surprised. Johnson said, "James, I'll admit you're pretty good, but you aren't good enough to hold up a novice."

James said, "Ellen's played a few times. Are you guys too chicken to play for beers?"

Roger looked at the
m speculatively, but Johnson snorted, "I generally don't like taking grad students' money but, I don't mind

taking *smart-assed* grad students' money. Lag for the break?"

James won the lag and broke, but didn't get anything in. Johnson promptly put three balls in.

Ell put in three to match him during her turn. Then, missing on purpose, she left Roger with a stymied leave. When she stepped back James whispered, "Why didn't you run the table?"

Ell turned to him and quietly said, "I told you I was just lucky that other night. You might have to buy some beer tonight."

James vehemently whispered back, "That was *not* luck!"

Ell shrugged and pointed to the pool table where Roger had missed his attempt at a bank shot, "Your turn."

James shook his head and went to look the table over. He put two balls in before giving himself a bad leave. Johnson stepped back up to the table, "I sure am getting thirsty, you two might want to go ahead and call a waitress over." He chalked his cue and promptly put in three more balls. For a few minutes Ell thought he was going to run out the table, but he missed a long cross table shot.

Ell took a deep breath and pondered just going ahead and missing her shot. She thought to herself that she shouldn't have gotten involved in this game with a man she didn't like. Especially, one who held power over her career. Then Johnson turned to James and quietly said, "Women can be good at math but, unlike men, they don't have the intuitive grasp of mechanics that you need for a game like this. You can see by the look on her face, she has no idea which shot to take."

Ell gritted her teeth, and then against her better

judgment, she put their remaining two balls in and turned to the eight ball. As the eight ball dropped she regretted her action and said with false brightness, "Jeez that was a lucky run!"

James had chills, every one of Ellen's balls had rolled smoothly into the very *center* of the pocket with a precision like he'd never seen before. Each leave was *perfect* for the next shot. With absolute certainty he knew there had been *no* luck whatsoever involved. Nonetheless he turned brightly to Roger and the Professor, "Hey, I guess you guys owe us a beer!"

Johnson scowled and turned to Roger, "I'll buy if you'll fetch." Roger headed to the bar and Johnson turned back to Ellen, intending to challenge another game, but she was on her way out the exit. He turned to James, "What got into her?"

James grinned, "We sandbagged you guys. She's actually really good at pool. But she said she needed to get home." He shrugged, "Women!"

Johnson's eyes narrowed as he looked after Ell, "She just got lucky! No way was that actual skill. Next time we're down here I'll want a rematch."

~~~

Ell spent the weekend thinking and running simulations. Saturday night she went into the lab to test a couple of predictions that she could run despite the faulty laser.

Monday morning it was back to double slit experiments. That afternoon at their three o'clock meeting she reported that her new apparatus demonstrated wavelike interference and documented field perturbations at both slits when a single high energy photon passed, apparently through *both* slits. To her this astonishing double slit result was a minor substantiation of her theory, far less important than what she was finding with her photon gluon resonance apparatus.

The other grad students looked at one another with wide eyes. To *them* it sounded like a result that could shake the world of physics!

Johnson though, rolled his eyes and said, "OK, there's got to be *something* wrong with your setup. I'll come and look at it after this meeting."

Ell said tentatively, "Uh, Dr. Johnson, I think you should let me tell you about some surprising results I got with my other setup."

"NO! Damn it! I am *not* interested in any weird results you're getting out of that spin bumping crap. Do not waste *my* time on it!" He sighed in dramatic exasperation, "It's bad enough that I have to spend time trying to figure out how you've screwed up the double slit apparatus."

He moved on to crucifying James over his experiment.

After the lab meeting Johnson came down to look at Ell's setup for the double slit experiment. She demonstrated the apparatus and he scratched his head as he looked it over and watched the flux detectors at both slits react to the passage of a single high energy photon. "Humph. I'm not sure what you're doing wrong. I'll have to think this over. Have you blocked access to one slit to make sure that the flux detector, on say the right slit, doesn't respond to passage of a photon through the left slit?"

"Yes sir. It doesn't."

"I'll think on it," he said, turning and walking out of the lab without another word.

When Johnson was gone Roger excitedly came over, "Let me see it! Do you think Donsaii might actually be right?!"

A little later James and Al came in too, also wanting to see her dual slit apparatus in action. The other grads wanted to go to West 87 to celebrate. Ell, dismayed by the loss of an evening working on her photon-gluon resonance apparatus, reluctantly agreed.

At Roger's urging she even had one sip of his beer for celebration. "You might be writing a paper crucifying some of the sacred cows of physics! You should call Donsaii and tell her you might have some supporting evidence!"

Ell nearly choked on her Coke. "Call Donsaii?" she laughed.

"Yeah! I'm sure she'd *love* to hear about some evidence that supports her theory. Wouldn't you like to talk to the genius herself?"

"Sure," Ell laughed, internally amused at the thought of speaking to herself. "But didn't you say you thought her theories were a bunch of crap?"

"In physics, your theory's only a bunch of crap until someone proves you're actually right!" He turned serious, "Uh, Ellen? You really should take Johnson's advice and drop that spin bumping stuff and focus on these dual slit results. They could *make* your career."

"Uh..." Ell contemplated for a moment trying to explain her photon-gluon resonance results to the other grads. But if it didn't pan out? She decided against it. "I need to get on my way, gotta get my beauty rest. Thanks for the Coke and the sip of beer."

Ell had actually intended to head back to the lab and spend some time setting up the new laser she'd picked up that morning. However, Roger got up when she did and said, "Let me walk you home."

Ell looked up at Roger and smiled, she liked him a lot. "Thanks. You *do* know I can find my way home by myself don't you?"

Roger shrugged self-consciously, "Yeah, but what if the Rigellians are active tonight?"

Ell raised her brows in surprise that James had told Roger about the "Rigellians," "Well, OK, then." She made a tiny curtsy and spoke with gravity, "I had entirely failed to take the Rigellians into consideration."

The walk home was pleasant despite the weather being pretty chilly. When they passed the That's Amore pizzeria Roger asked, "Hey, you want to go in for a slice? I'll buy."

Ell realized she was pretty hungry, so, even though it delayed her getting back to the lab, she said "OK."

They went in and got a table.

As they waited, Ell asked Roger about his childhood and was stunned to learn that he was from Morehead City! Ell realized that her high school classmate Shelly Emmerit must be Roger's younger sister and that Ell had eaten in his family's restaurant many times. He ran a hand through his bushy hair, "You know Morehead City's where Ell Donsaii grew up don't you?"

"Um, yeah, I think I heard that."

"My sister even knew her, they were classmates. I've been hoping I might somehow get to meet her one of the times that I'm back home, but she's not in Morehead City very often. Maybe I'll see her over Christmas break? I did go to a talk she gave, but there were so many people there that there was no way I could meet her."

"Wait a minute. I thought you thought she was crazy?"

"Johnson said that, not me. *I* said her 'math was incomprehensible.'"

"Wait..." Ell frowned, "she gave a talk?" Ell wondered what talk he could be referring to.

"Yeah, she spoke at the high school graduation this summer."

Goosebumps went up Ell's spine; she'd never considered that someone like Roger might be there for the speech she gave at graduation. "Uh, what'd she talk about?" Ell felt she needed to ask, in order to maintain her separate identity, but she also wondered if he'd paid attention.

"Believe it or not, she talked about the double slit experiment." He raised an eyebrow. "Told the audience we should *all* work on it. I *know* she'd be excited to hear about your results. You really should contact her."

"Maybe when I have more confidence in the results. What if Johnson finds a mistake?"

"Yeah, I guess you should wait a little. But I'd like to be there when you tell her."

"Um, you really seem interested in her?"

"Yeah. She's really, really smart, she likes physics and she's *gorgeous*. What's not to like?"

Ell was amused to find that she felt simultaneously complimented as "Ell" and hurt as "Ellen." On one hand, she realized that her sentiment was unfair; she'd actually asked Gloria to make her unattractive. She shouldn't be hurt if it'd worked. On the other hand, shouldn't Roger like her for her mind and not for her looks? "Hmmm, Roger, what am I, chopped liver?"

~~~

Roger ducked his head shyly. "No, Ellen. You're great. I really like you a lot. But I've got to admit I've got

Smarter

some serious hero worship for Donsaii. I wish Johnson wasn't so down on her; I'd kinda like to work on some of the predictions her theory makes myself." He chuckled, "At least, I'd like to work on it if I have you around to help me understand that weird math. When I first read her paper I thought it was so far out there as to verge on the ridiculous. It wasn't until Johnson had you explain the paper to us that I started to understand the math and admire Donsaii for physics instead of gymnastics."

Roger suddenly realized he hardly ever thought about Ellen's odd appearance anymore. She was his friend. He became conscious of the fact that he'd like it if she were... more than a friend.

The pizza came and Roger watched as Ellen wolfed down a couple slices. He'd often been astonished at how much she ate; thinking that if she just cut back a little, her butt might not be quite so big. Though, now as he sat across a table from her, looking at only her upper half, he realized that she didn't actually look overweight at all. Strangely enough it really was all in her hips. *Well,* he thought to himself, *I don't* care *if her butt's too big, I like her the way she is.*

~~~

Ell found it strange, eating with a Roger who seemed so intensely focused on her tonight. She'd been finding his quiet intensity more and more attractive, but she'd never expected to find it focused on her. *Or was it? Could I just be imagining he's attracted to Ellen with the big butt and beaky nose?*

Pizza finished, they started walking the rest of the way back to Ell's apartment. Roger asked about her childhood and Ell told him briefly about "Ellen's" imaginary life before NCSU. Their hands bumped. To her surprise, Roger's hand gently grasped hers and they walked on, hand in hand, Ell wondering just what holding hands meant in this situation. Ell began to worry about what he might expect when they got to her apartment. To her relief, when she'd opened the gate to the complex and turned to him, he bent and gently pecked her on the cheek. "Good night, Ellen, and congratulations on your experiment." Throatily he said, "Someday, I imagine I'll be telling my kids I knew you." He turned and walked off into the evening.

Ell went upstairs to get a change of clothes, and then started back to the lab, eager to start her new photon-gluon resonance experiments. She spent the night in the lab, sleeping a few hours in intermittent catnaps on the lab's cot, getting more and more excited about her results until it became almost impossible to get back to sleep. It really did look like she could send information from one entangled macromolecule to the other. She'd been able to confirm that information transmitted even when the receiver apparatus was in a Faraday cage so it couldn't be occurring through some odd radio effect. Because it transmitted an "event" when the laser went on and off, she should be able to send very large files of binary information the same way it was done in fiber optic communication systems. She needed to be able to separate her sending and receiving elements farther than she could by just carting the receiver down the hall to be more confident that some other physical effect wasn't responsible for the data transmission. After some excited thought she realized that she should be able to make very small units with the circuit fabrication equipment available in the Physics department's fab lab. By seven the next morning she'd designed a circuit and a chip with an off the shelf optoelectronic laser set to stimulate her entangled carbon nanotube, sending data as if it were going to stream into a normal fiber optic fiber.

In a bout of paranoia, before she sent the design file down to the circuit fab to construct a pair of her devices she struck a couple of bridge connections from the design. This left a circuit that should apparently function, but would deliver an incorrect voltage to the EM field and appeared to use the laser only for heating. But two solder bridges would restore it to her intended design. Then she had Allan record all the details of the bench top setup. Once she was sure she could reassemble her bench top setup, she switched a number of things around, hooking the input up to the magnetic field and the laser to a simple power source. She modified settings and the laser frequency until there was no chance it would work. Then she looked at it for a few moments, wondering what had made her want to modify it so it wouldn't work? No one knew about it, so no one could come in and try to steal her idea could they?

She shook her head and set out to get breakfast and teach her introductory physics lab.

Chapter Seven

By the time she'd finished teaching the lab and stopped back by, the fab lab had finished her devices. When she arrived back in the research lab Johnson was sitting, staring at her dual slit apparatus, chin resting on his doubled fists. "Hi, Dr. Johnson." She said brightly. "Have you found any problems with my setup?"

Without looking up he simply said, "No."

"Do you want me to start writing it up?"

"No."

"Um, OK. Why not?"

"There *is* something wrong with it," he said, irritatedly. "I just haven't figured out *what* yet. I don't intend to be embarrassed by a paper where someone else has to tell me what you did wrong. First thing we need to do is replicate this with a completely different setup. Instead of 100 series flux detectors use the 109s, they're better. Put Faraday cages around both of them to eliminate interference. Set up with a different emitter that can generate several different photon energy levels to see if you get similar results at different energies."

"Yes sir, will do… Uh, I'd like to tell you ab…"

He interrupted her, "Next, my AI tells me you ordered a couple of chip circuits constructed by the fab this morning."

"Uh, yes sir." A chill went over her at his glacial tone.

"They were *very* expensive and I'm willing to bet that they're for your spin bumping bullhockey?"

"Uh, yes sir. I can pay for them if you want."

"Damn *right* you'll pay for them. I've let you slide on some small items you've charged to the lab. Things I suspected were for that crap but didn't cost very much. However, now I'm *done* paying for this wild hare you've got up your ass. Make a transfer into the lab account to cover them *and* any other crap you've bought on our account by this afternoon." He got up and left the lab without seeing Ell's white face.

~~~

Roger was appalled by the way Johnson had treated Ellen and even more worried as minutes passed with her still standing where she'd been when Johnson left the lab. He got up and walked over, putting his hand on her shoulder. When he did, she moved convulsively. Ellen violently struck his hand from her shoulder and dropped to a crouch. She stared at him wide eyed from the crouch. "Oh, Roger, I'm so sorry!" At least that's what he thought she said; the words were a rapid fire burst and he could hardly separate one word from another.

~~~

Ell desperately tried to damp herself back down out of the zone her rage had sent her into. With dismay she saw Roger rubbing his wrist where she'd struck it. She gradually stood back up, and, carefully slowing her speech down to what she hoped was normal, she said, "Roger, I'm so sorry. I was *really* pissed and you startled me. Did I hurt your wrist?"

"I'll be fine," he said, amazed by how badly his wrist

hurt. "I'm sorry too. He shouldn't treat you that way."

"Well," she took a deep breath, then sighed, "I did charge stuff to his account."

"*Everybody* does that if they have side projects. You're the *only* one he's ever called on it."

"Still, I was in the wrong... Fred," she said to her "Ellen" AI. "Figure out what I've charged to the Johnson account for my sideline experiments and make a transfer... Oh!" She grimaced. "Wow, I didn't think they'd be that much. I guess it's no surprise he was pissed. OK, transfer some money out of my savings then." She looked back at Roger who was still rubbing his wrist. "You sure you're OK?"

"Oh! Yeah sure." he said, dropping his wrist. "Hey if you need any more circuits from the fab, you should talk to Emma, she's a wizard at saving money by using off the shelf components, no matter what you're designing."

"Um, I should have thought of that. Thanks. Well I'd better get to re-setting this double slit apparatus."

Roger looked at her pensively for a moment, "You might want to talk to Dr. Sponchesi. He's *really* nice and very smart. Maybe not in Johnson's league for brilliance but a great guy. He might be able to advise you on how to deal with Johnson, or publish your paper yourself... or something."

"Thanks, I'll ask Emma about him when I talk to her about my circuit. Working in his lab she'll probably have some idea how he'd respond."

~~~

At the lab meeting that afternoon Ell reported that she hadn't finished the revised setup for the double slit experiment. "But I'll get it done tonight." She finished.

"Tonight?" Johnson grated. "I thought your nights were reserved for your harebrained spin bumping experiments?"

"Uh, yes sir. But I have some things to do on my own experiment that have to be done during the day over the next couple of days. So, I'll work on the double slit tonight to make up for it."

Johnson eyed her for a moment, jaw twitching as if he wanted to say something more, but then he turned to Roger.

~~~

That night Ell finished revising the setup on the new double slit experiment and ran it a couple of times, getting the same results as with the first setup. She sent Johnson a message with the results. Then she turned to her new circuits and solder bridged the faults she'd built into the design. Then she used the micromanipulator to pick out a pair of nanotubes that should resonate with the frequency of the laser in the opto circuits. She confirmed that they did, entangled and installed them. She hooked up the first one to a data output from her AI. In a fit of historical whimsy she sent Alexander Graham Bell's first phone message, "Mr. Watson, come here." Her heart trip-hammered in her chest as she saw the message appear on the display screen hooked up to the second device! She realized that she was so excited that she'd slipped into her zone. It took several long calming breaths to get her back out of it.

Ell left one PGR, as she was calling the photon-gluon resonance circuits, hooked up to the signal from the national atomic clock and headed back to her apartment for a shower. The entire walk back she was able to see the signal from the clock on her second PGR.

Since the first PGR wasn't running on enough power to transmit a radio signal all the way to her apartment, this was pretty good proof that the signal was actually being transmitted by PGR.

There was no way for her to determine whether the transmission was instantaneous or merely light speed as yet, so she went to bed and, after some restless thrashing, got almost her usual three hours of sleep. When she woke up she went online and submitted an IDF or "Invention Disclosure Form" to the NCSU Office of Technology Transfer. She also placed a request for an appointment in their office, then she headed out to meet Emma for her run.

"Hey, where were you yesterday? I had to run by myself, in constant fear of the Rigellians." Emma grinned at her.

Ell laughed; James' Rigellians were gaining fame. "Sorry, I slept over in the lab last night. Finally having some luck with my experiment."

"Arggh! Mine's going horribly. I will seek my revenge by running you into the ground this morning."

Ell said, "Sorry, I know what that's like. Can I help?"

"Hey, great idea. Could you check my math on my new experiment for me?"

"OK, while I'm doing that maybe you could look at a circuit I built that turns out to be really expensive. Roger says you're a wizard at designing cheap circuits."

"OK, but I'm still going to kill you on this run." She turned and jogged off into the early morning mist. Despite her threatening words she was supportive during the run, cajoling Ell to run farther and faster than she thought she could.

Smarter

~~~

Ell found two minor errors in Emma's math which were probably responsible for her frustrating results. However, Emma managed a circuit redesign that cut the cost of Ell's circuit a hundredfold by using existing microchip circuits for almost all of it. It was also much smaller. Ell was ecstatic and immediately submitted a request for five pairs of them.

Fred, her AI said, "Dr. Johnson wants to know, 'Where the hell you are?'"

"Tell him I'm on my way to the lab."

When Ell arrived, Johnson barked, "Where the hell have you been?"

"Sir, I was helping Emma Kenner from the Sponchesi lab... She helped me with my project at the same time."

"I assume that by 'my project' you mean your ridiculous pursuit of spin bumping?"

"Yes sir, though I've given up on spin bumping per se and..."

"Don't waste my time explaining it."

"But I..."

"*Don't!* I thought you'd promised me that you'd only waste time on it evenings and weekends."

"Yes sir," Ell bit out. "But you'll remember that I worked on the dual slit experiment last night so that I could have some daylight hours to work on my project."

He studied her, "But all you did last night was get the dual slit experiment to fail."

"No sir. It worked."

"What the hell do you mean it worked? It's still reporting flux at both slits when a single photon passes!"

"Yes sir! Which is exactly what m... m... what Donsaii's equations predict!"

He rolled his eyes. "That's a bunch of crap. You're *doing* something wrong! Don't wait for *me* to figure it out for you. Get in here and figure out what you're doing wrong yourself. There's a limit to just how much hand holding I can do around here." He spun on his heel and exited.

After Johnson left, Roger came over, carefully this time. This time he didn't touch Ellen before he spoke quietly, "There is nothing more horrific in science than the murder of a dearly held hypothesis by that dastardly fiend, data."

Ellen shoulders slumped and she turned to Roger, suddenly burying her face in his chest, "*Why* does he hate me?"

Roger awkwardly put his arms around her and gently squeezed. "He doesn't *hate* you. He hates *Donsaii*, I think, and her brilliant equations. He really doesn't want them to be right."

Ell snuffled into his shirt. "Same thing." She said enigmatically, without elaborating on the double meaning.

~~~

Ell dutifully studied her double slit apparatus a few minutes, pondering whether she could, in fact, have overlooked some flaw, decided that she hadn't and spent another half hour pulling her preliminary notes together into a paper ready for submission. She sent it to Johnson's inbox and went downstairs to pick up her new PGRs. On the way back Fred notified her that she had an appointment in the Tech Transfer Office at 1PM with a Mr. Wayne Stillman. She went back to the lab and put nanotubes in all of her new PGRs and tested them to be sure they worked.

Smarter

They didn't!

In a panic she reviewed Emma's design and with some relief realized that Emma had replicated the faults Ell had built into the first design. It was extremely difficult to micro-solder the tiny bridges on Emma's smaller design, but Ell got it done on one pair. Once the bridges were soldered, that pair worked fine. She solder bridged the rest of them.

Ell checked a pair of small picosecond accurate clocks out of the equipment room, synched them exactly, and hooked one up to the input of one PGR and the other clock to a micro AI which was also attached to the second PGR. That way the AI could measure the difference between the readings of the two clocks. She put the first clock-PGR combo into a doubled FedEx box and addressed it to Australia with instructions on the inner box to mail it back to her apartment. Not a perfect experiment, but about as cheaply as she could think to check for light speed delays.

Another pair of PGRs she used to hook Allan, her AI, up to the net through one of the lab's computers. Months ago, she'd modified the power switch on her AI so that flipping the power switch turned off the outer case lights but left the actual AI running. She'd also installed a microphone inside the case so that Allan could hear what was happening around him without being jacked to the AI headband. Thus Allan was already able to report to the police and her family if something happened to Ell.

But with the PGR connection, Allan would be able to reach the net even if someone kidnapped her while using a net jammer!

Roger's chair scraped back and he said, "Hey busy lady, wanna grab some lunch?"

Ell looked up, surprised to see it was noon and said, "Sure!" She picked up her FedEx box and a couple of her PGRs and they headed out.

Roger said, "What'cha sending?" nodding at the FedEx box.

"Hmmm, a little experiment."

"You can't send our equipment to someone else! You're in enough trouble over using the fab, aren't you?"

"It's going out and coming back. Nothing's actually going to anyone else. I'd rather not talk about it. How's your experiment going?"

"Going out and coming back?"

"How's your experiment going?" She grinned crookedly up at him.

He snorted, "Crappy as usual. The output is a factor of 6 lower than it should be."

"Hmmm, 'There is nothing more horrific in science than the murder of a dearly held hypothesis by dastardly data.'"

"Hey! I was being nice to you and accusing *Johnson* of being wedded to a hypothesis. Now you're throwing it up to *me*?"

"No, but I'm wondering if the output is only low because it's rotated to your receiver."

"What? Rotated how?"

"Because, if your hypothesis is wrong, according to Donsaii's theory the output should be polarized and if it *is* polarized, but rotated differently than that big ass polarizer filter you've got on the front of your receiver you'd lose most of your signal reception."

Roger stopped stock still on the stairs, staring off into space. Then he turned and started climbing the stairs again.

Ell said, "Hey, where are you going?"

"Back up to rotate my big ass polarizer filter!"

"What about my lunch?"

"You'll have to eat it by yourself."

"But, aren't you going to buy me lunch for figuring out what's wrong with your experiment?"

He stopped, grinned down at her, then turned and descended again. "A man must eat. I'll turn it later. But I'm *not* buying you lunch until you're proven right!"

"Oh ho! You *know* I am. I'll charge you interest on lunch tomorrow by having a dessert too!"

~~~

They ate in the cafeteria. Ell put her package in the FedEx pick up bin on her way out of the building. As she was walking to the tech transfer office Allan came on and said, "You have a call from Phillip Zabrisk."

"Put him on! Phil, what brings you to call? You broke and needing a loan?"

Phil's voice said, "Exactly. I'm coming home next week for Thanksgiving and thought I'd see if I could get you to buy my broke ass another lunch?"

"Great! Call me when you get free from the family and I'll meet you somewhere."

They spoke a while longer, catching up, but Ell had to hang up when she was called in for her appointment in the tech office.

~~~

"Ms… Symonds, is it?" the small man behind the desk said, looking at his screen.

"Yes sir."

"And you work in Dr. Albert Johnson's lab in Physics, a first year grad student?"

"Yes sir."

"Yet you haven't listed Dr. Johnson on your invention disclosure form?"

"It doesn't have a blank for my professor."

"Ah," Stillman said with a condescending tone, "but any intellectual property you have developed has been under his guidance and mentorship."

"No sir."

"What do you mean, 'no'?"

"He has specifically and repeatedly denied me guidance or assistance on this particular project and denied me the use of any University funding for it. He has, in fact, frequently told me to stop wasting time on it. I've compiled an audio-video file of those conversations that my AI is sending to your AI—now. I've used University facilities and equipment evenings and nights otherwise I could argue that the University has no interest in this intellectual property."

"Oh you could, could you?" His tone segued to mildly threatening.

"Yes sir. But I'm *not* arguing that. The University itself has provided some support."

"Hmmm, and you claim it's based on Ell Donsaii's quantum theory?

"Yes sir."

"But you don't believe she has any rights to this invention due to her development of the theory?"

"No sir. The discoverer of a principle does not, therefore, own rights to all devices based on that principle. Ms. Donsaii didn't patent *use* of the principle."

"Hmmm. And you claim that it will allow communication between two points, but no others? Kind of like a walkie talkie?"

"Yes sir." Ell had a feeling that this man couldn't actually see the potential of such a device. She began to wonder if she'd have to point out its uses to him.

"Well, I'm sorry Ms. Symonds. I've already spoken to Dr. Johnson. He tells me that this project of yours is an *absolute* dead end based entirely on wishful fantasies on your part. The University would not want to put any resources behind an attempt to commercialize something like this."

Ell rocked back, stunned by Stillman's short sightedness. For a moment she considered showing him the working model, but realized that he'd likely deny the evidence before his own eyes in favor of testimony from Dr. Johnson. He seemed to believe that its ability to send messages to only one receiver was a problem, not an advantage. "So… then you'll turn the rights to the invention back over to me and… I'll… I'll have to patent it myself?"

"Well, that has to be approved by our committee, but essentially that's what I expect will happen. The University may keep a 5% interest, just in case you're actually able to make a useful device from your concept, but it won't invest any more of its resources into development. The committee meets on Friday so we should be able to let you know then."

Laurence E Dahners

Chapter Eight

Ell wandered back to the physics building in a daze, somewhat ecstatic that NCSU would likely grant her most or all of the rights to her invention rather than only 40% of any royalty stream as per their usual, but daunted by the need to commercialize it all by herself. "Allan, please see if I can speak to Dr. Smythe at MIT?"

She was nearly back to the physics building when Smythe came on line. "Ell, great to hear from you! Sorry to say though, we've been unable to get diddly going using spin bumping. Are you and Al having any luck?"

For a moment Ell was confused, and then remembered that Dr. Johnson's first name was "Albert" and Dr. Smythe would be referring to him, not Al the grad student in the Johnson's lab. "Uh, no sir. No luck. In fact, Dr. Johnson forbade me working on it except evenings and weekends. I have had some luck with photon-gluon resonance though."

"Oh no! Is Al one of those guys who's pleasant at meetings, but a real curmudgeon at home?"

"Uhhh..."

"Don't sugar coat it. Go ahead and tell me if that's what's going on. Al and I may be friends but... I'd like to think that you and I are friends too."

"Uh. Yes sir. Most of the grad students find him pretty harsh I'd say. My particular problem is that he's entirely focused on disproving those crazy Donsaii theories and really doesn't want to hear about anything that conflicts with his world view. He's had me working on dual slit and our current setup shows single photons creating flux at both slits which he *really* doesn't want to hear about."

"Flux! What? Tell me about this."

Ell explained their high energy photon setup and the results they were getting using the new flux detection technology. Smythe interrupted repeatedly with perceptive questions.

She continued, "But, Dr. Johnson's still trying to figure out what's wrong with the experimental setup because he's sure the results can't be correct."

"Well he's in the right there. 'Extraordinary claims require extraordinary evidence' and all that. But—that's phenomenal! Be sure you do everything you can think of to make sure you haven't made a mistake before you publish, but if you don't find a problem with your setup you're gonna be famous in physics! Let me suggest..." Dr. Smythe went on to suggest several refinements to their setup that Ell thought were amazingly perceptive. Then he said, "But you were going to tell me about— was it photon-gluon resonance?"

"Yes sir, I've been working on it nights and weekends and I've been able to send a digital signal from one entangled molecule to another."

"My God! How? No, don't tell me. That would be incredibly valuable IP. Your university's going to make a fortune. You too I suppose, depending on how they do their royalties?"

For a moment Ell puzzled over "IP" then realized it was short for "Intellectual Property." She said, "Well, yes sir. That's the issue. Normally the inventor gets 40% of the royalty stream. But I've become kind of a *persona non grata* with Dr. Johnson because I keep working on this resonance phenomenon. He told the university my IP's without merit, so they're probably going to return the rights to me. They might keep 5%, but they won't help me patent or commercialize. That means I need to find funding for a patent and a company to commercialize it myself."

"Holy shee...! Don't they know who they're dealing with? Oops, no I guess they don't. You're working under your pseudonym aren't you?"

"Uh, yes sir."

"Do you want me to call them up and tell them what idiots they're being?"

"Un, no sir. I'm not happy here, so I think I'll probably leave NCSU pretty soon anyway... though I would like to submit the dual slit paper first. I was actually calling you hoping you can help me make some contacts with folks that could help me commercialize?"

"Well, you'd have to have a working model of a communication device to get much traction with industry. An esoteric lab bench setup can be a hard sell, even if Al would let you bring people in to look at it. How close are you to trying to design and build something close to what might be made commercially?

"Um, I have four prototype pairs."

"What? You *have* been busy! How big are they?"

"Ten by ten by seventeen millimeters."

"Your *prototypes* are that small? And they work?!"

"Uh, yes sir. They're really pretty simple. Once you understand the principles involved, that is. We used a lot of off the shelf chip tech."

"We? I thought you said Johnson wasn't involved?"

"No sir. But one of the other grad students is a tech wizard and she helped me design the second set of physical prototypes. The ones I made myself were much larger and a *lot* more expensive. I bought time on the circuit fab here in the department to make both my original prototype and the better ones Emma helped me design."

"You bought? Johnson's making you spend your *own* money on this project?"

"Yes sir. He's repeatedly told me to 'stop wasting time' on it."

"Well... I guess if you worked on it nights and weekends and paid for supplies yourself, you *should* own it. Or at least most of it. Damn right! I'll touch base with a couple of venture capital folks I know here in Boston. I think they'll be interested. Can I tell them your real name?"

"I think I should wait on that until we know whether NCSU is going to keep rights to the invention or not. It may be that if I'm commercializing something that's partly owned by the U it'd be simpler to do it as Ellen Symonds."

"OK, I'll try to set up something for December, maybe the..." there was a pause as he checked a calendar, "the 12th. Will you have any finals or anything that would keep you from being able to make it then?"

"No, sir. I'm not even sure I'll still be enrolled here at State then."

"Oh, wow, you *do* sound unhappy. Well, remember, if you think you can be safe here at MIT, we can still make a spot for you."

"Thank you, sir. And thanks also for any help you can give me making industry contacts. Is there *any* way I can repay you?"

"Hah! Sure, endow my research when you're rich!"

Ell's eyebrows drew together. "Do you really think

this will be worth that much?"

"Oh my god! You haven't thought too much about the possible applications have you?"

"Well, some."

"Hmmm, consider that if it really works, and works reliably, it should be able to replace radio, fiberoptic and wired data transmission in almost all of our civilization's communications systems."

"Ohhh, that *is* a big industry isn't it?"

"Yes, and there are a lot of other applications. Think about them and make a list for your prospective buyers. Just be sure that your prototypes really work and work reliably before you show up for a demo in December. It'd be embarrassing for both of us if they didn't perform as claimed. In fact, I'd truly appreciate the chance to evaluate them myself before we put them in front of possible buyers. Is there any chance you could visit Boston before then so I can see them in action?"

"I'll... try to work it out."

"Great!"

After she hung up, Ell focused back on her surroundings and found herself standing outside the Physics building. She went in and up to the lab where she checked the PGR that was hooked up to the clock in the FedEx box. It still showed a steady reading with no detectable difference between the readings of the two clocks, so she put the PGR-clock in her pocket. She queried FedEx for the location of the package and found that the other member of the pair was across town at the FedEx terminal awaiting shipment.

Ell modified the dual slit apparatus per Smythe's suggestions and reran the test with the same results, then altered the description of the setup in the paper and sent it to Johnson again. She checked her bank account and found to her dismay that she had burned through most of the savings she'd put away while at the Academy! She leaned back in her chair and tried to figure out how to handle all the things she had on the burner with so little cash available.

Roger saw her come in, work a little with her devices and then sit, staring up into space. He wondered what was going on. After a bit he came over and asked, "Ellen? Everything OK?"

"Huh? Oh, yeah. I'm just trying to plan out some things in my head here."

"How's your experiment going?"

"Both are doing good. Was I right about your polarization filter?"

"Yeah, Thanks! I really appreciate your figuring out what was happening, though you messed up my hypothesis big time."

"Hey, no problem. And don't get too down in the dumps; you know some of science's biggest advances come from things that don't turn out the way they're supposed to? You just have to figure out what it means, even if it doesn't fit your original hypothesis."

"Uh, you should know that Johnson was here in the lab when I got back from lunch. I should have told you before. He was here messing with your stuff long before he called you this morning too. He was pissed the first time, but even more pissed the second time."

"Really? He spent all that time on the dual slit apparatus? It's pretty simple to run and gives the same results every time. Was he running a lot of different photon energies or something? Or could you tell?"

"No he actually spent most of his time looking at your other setup. The one for your spin bumping study. Do you think he's coming around to thinking there's a chance that might work?"

A chill went down Ell's spine. "Hmmm, somehow I doubt it. Maybe we'll find out at the lab meeting in a little while." Ell picked up the rest of her PGR circuits from beside her bench top apparatus and put them in her pocket. Thank goodness for the baggy clothing she wore over her fat pants. Then she resumed staring into space until three o'clock rolled around and they headed to the meeting.

At the meeting, Johnson was in a real mood. He grilled Al on his experiment for a couple minutes and then turned to Ell with fire in his eyes. "And just what in all the hells do you think you're doing?"

"I'm trying to write up the dual slit experiment. Have you found an error yet?"

"No! Though there has to be *something* wrong, I haven't tumbled to it yet. But, I'm referring to your reporting an invention to the tech office?"

"Yes sir. My entanglement project has been fruitful, so I submitted a report so that the University could decide whether to commercialize it."

"First of all, it hasn't been fruitful, I looked it over this morning and it's a jumbled mess! It certainly isn't capable of transmitting data like you reported. Second, if you did have something to report, it would need to be cleared through me as your supervisor!"

Ell's eyes flashed in return, "Sir, I have on numerous occasions tried to tell you that that project *was* bearing fruit. You have *repeatedly* told me you didn't want to 'hear anything about that crap.' You've required that I work on it on my own time, using my own funds. I have compiled an audio-video record documenting those repeated demands on your part, which my AI has just forwarded to yours. You, therefore, are *not* my supervisor on that project; I've been running it completely on my own. I only reported it to the University because I've been doing it in their building while using equipment I checked out from their storeroom."

Johnson rocked back. None of his students had ever given him this kind of backtalk before! He couldn't believe that a grad student in her first semester was mouthing off! He leaned back forward and ground out, "I helped you set up your first spin bumping apparatus!"

"Spin bumping never worked. Photon-gluon resonance is what worked and that's what I reported to the tech office."

"What!? You didn't mention anything about photon-gluon resonance!"

"I asked permission to tell you about it in one of our lab meetings, you said, and I quote, 'No! Damn it! I am *not* interested in any weird results you are getting out of that crap. Don't waste my time on it! It's bad enough that I have to spend time trying to figure out how you've screwed up the double slit apparatus.'" Ell took a deep breath, and continued in a quiet, calm tone, "Therefore, I continued working on it by myself."

Johnson stared at her for a moment, then said, "Photon-gluon resonance? Sounds like some malarkey you just made up."

"It's also predicted by Donsaii's equations."

"All that aside. It doesn't work. I tried it out this morning. It has a terrible feedback loop in it for God's sake!

"Yes, once I realized that it represented a valuable intellectual property, I disabled and rewired it to protect that property."

"That's a load of crap! The rest of this lab meeting is cancelled." Glaring, he rose to his feet. "You and I are going to go down and you are going to *show* me just what you *think* your setup can do!"

The rest of the grad students were appalled. They glanced back and forth at each other, completely dismayed at the way Ellen was being treated, but fully expecting her to go along with Johnson in order to save her position.

Instead, Ellen remained seated, eyes flashing while she took several deep breaths. She trembled, not as if she were in fear as they expected, but rather as if she were very, very angry. One more long deep breath, then she calmly said, "You, sir, are a tyrant and a bully. *You* may believe that your behavior in dealing with your students is acceptable, but it has not been. That kind of behavior is not tolerable in modern human society. I hereby notify you that I am resigning my position in your lab. I also notify you that I intend to submit the dual slit paper; do you wish to withdraw your name from it?"

"You can't submit that paper without my permission!"

"There is no law in science that says I have to have my supervisor's permission to submit a paper. I will simply note that you do not approve it. When it's published, others will attempt to replicate my results. I am confident they'll obtain the same findings and the paper will be judged on its merits, with or *without* your approval."

"Do as you like with that paper. But you'll demonstrate this photon-gluon resonance phenomenon to me now or I'll be writing such scathing letters that you'll be lucky to hire on as a janitor!"

Smarter

To the astonishment of the other students Ellen's eyes crinkled, then she laughed! She calmly stood and said, "Do your worst. I believe the world will be more interested in my results than your letters. I'll be heading over to the admin office now to formalize my resignation." She turned and swept the other grad students with her eyes, "Good luck to you guys. Sorry to leave on such a note." She turned and walked out the door. As her chair was nearest the door, she was well down the hall before Johnson made it out the door himself and, still seething with frustration, watched her turn into the stairwell.

~~~

On her way home Ell sent Dr. Smythe a message that she could visit Boston with a prototype for his evaluation any time the rest of that week or the next as long as she was back before Thanksgiving.

She didn't want to miss seeing Phil when he was home in North Carolina.

~~~

Once she was back in her apartment she submitted the dual slit paper to Nature with a letter noting that one of the investigators did not accept the results and had withdrawn his name from the paper.

Allan said, "You have a call from Dr. Smythe."

Excitedly Ell said, "Put him on... Hello Dr. Smythe."

"Hi Ell. How are you able to get away to Boston so soon?"

In an unhappy tone, she said, "I've resigned here at NCSU."

"Oh!" He paused, then said somberly, "I'm *so* sorry to hear that. Well, come on up tomorrow or the next day. You can tell me about it and we'll put your prototype through the mill here in the lab."

"OK, I'll make a reservation and let you know."

~~~

Once she had plane reservations for the morning and had notified Smythe, Ell sat back, realizing that she felt immensely better and more relaxed, even though she was worried about the cost of flying to Boston. She decided Johnson's constant harassment must have been bothering her more than she'd thought. Allan said, "You have a call from Roger Emmerit."

Ell felt a little glow at that, and took the call. "Roger, how're you holding up without me to reorient your polarizer?"

He sounded depressed, "OK, I guess Ellen, but we all miss having you around. Are you OK?"

"Oh yeah! I feel great just getting away from Johnson. Sorry you're still under his thumb."

"We're wondering if we can buy you dinner, now that you have no visible means of support?"

"Sure! A girl's gotta eat you know."

"Meet us at That's Amore?"

"When?"

"Now."

When Ell walked into Amore she saw Roger, Emma and James sitting forlornly at a table in the corner. "Hey guys."

"Hey." They said together, sounding as if they were at a funeral.

"You guys this depressed just because you miss my scintillating company?"

Emma said, "Ell, don't make light of it. The guys told

me about the row you had with Johnson. He's a vindictive SOB and really will do his best to destroy your career. I think you should come talk to Dr. Sponchesi. He's really nice."

James put a hand on hers, "You really should consider putting your tail between your legs and apologizing to Johnson. He ruined another grad student's career a few years back. That was after they got in a lot less of a fight than this one."

Ell looked around at their long faces, "I'm gonna be OK, believe it or not. I really am." Their waiter came to take an order then, defusing the moment. They managed to share a large pizza without any more dramatic conversation. They even got a few laughs in, Roger being particularly tickled about the look on Johnson's face when Ellen called him a "tyrant and a bully."

He snorted, "Then you should have seen him rampaging through your stuff back in the lab. He took pictures of your setup from every angle, then cussed at it while disassembling and reassembling parts of it. When I left he was still in full storm mode. I hope you didn't have any design files on the departmental computer systems. I'm pretty sure he spent some time looking in your folders there too."

"No, everything to do with that project has been stored solely on my AI ever since he told me I could only work on it nights and weekends." Ell worried a little about the design files for her prototypes which would be stored on the department's server. Even though she'd modified them to be nonfunctional without the solder bridges, she worried they might provide clues.

After a while they broke up, Ell agreeing to meet Emma for their run in the morning and to join James for pool some time at West 87. Roger walked her home and shortly into their walk Ell was pleased to find that Roger had managed to slip her hand into his again. At her apartment complex he turned and gave her a hug. She again had mixed feelings of relief that he wasn't trying to come up to her apartment and disappointment that he wasn't... Roger held the hug for a bit, and then whispered in her ear, "If you ever need anything. Just let me know. I'd surely like to remain your friend." He leaned his head back to look into her eyes.

Ell found she had a frog in her throat. She nodded, momentarily unable to speak, then managed to croak, "Always, my good buddy. Always." She cleared her throat, "We'll see each other some more, don't you worry." She was touched to see his eyes shimmering a bit.

~~~

Roger leaned his head back beside hers, afraid she'd see his watery eyes and wondering if he dared try to kiss her. He started to pull his head back to give it a try. At the last moment he chickened out, gave her a squeeze and pecked her on the cheek, then turned quickly to head back down the street.

~~~

Ell watched Roger walk away, hands jammed in his pockets. She wondered if she was destined to remain un-kissed forever? She was eighteen for God's sake! Shouldn't she have some kind of a love life by now? She trudged upstairs. As she arrived in her apartment, Allan said, "You have a call from your mother."

"Put her on." Then trying to put some pep in her

voice she brightly said, "Hi, Mom."

There was a moment of silence, then Ell realized her mother was sobbing. "Hi, Ell." Ell heard her choke. "I'm so sorry…"

"Oh no. What's happened? Is it Gram?" Her grandmother's health wasn't the greatest.

"No, no. We're all OK. It's that SOB Jake. Of course I have no access to our joint accounts. Now he's managed to tie up the little bit of money in my own accounts. The divorce attorney is costing a fortune and, with your Gram living on a fixed income, I really hate to ask her. Now my car broke down and the attorney's demanding some cash up front because he's not sure we'll be able to get much out of Jake in any divorce settlement. It's humiliating to ask my daughter, but I thought I'd see what your current financial situation is? Would you be able to loan me a few thousand?"

Ell felt like her world had just crashed in. So many problems at once. "Oh, Mom! That's terrible. Right now I could loan you that much and then re-up with the Air Force. But, then I'd be broke and have no income. I just quit here at NCSU."

"You did? Why?"

Ell gave her a brief synopsis.

"But you think this invention of yours will bring in some money?"

"Well, I hope so, but it'll be quite a while. And I probably need to take out loans to apply for patents and… I don't know what else. I'll get to work applying for some kind of loan immediately."

Her mother responded, sounding like she'd gained some resolve. "No! Don't do that yet. I'll ask your Gram about the state of her savings. If she's got any cushion at all, I know she'll help me so you can try to make a success out of your invention."

They spoke a few more minutes about what a jerk Jake was. After they hung up, Ell pondered with some surprise how quickly her mother had trusted her about the invention. She thought most parents would have serious doubts about the likelihood of their child ever inventing anything successful.

***

Ell, traveling as "Ellen," got out of the autotaxi in front of the Physics building at MIT and made her way into the lobby. Before she went upstairs, Ell checked with FedEx to determine the location of her package and learned that it'd finally arrived in Perth. She took a deep breath, if the transmission from one PGR to the other was at the speed of light there should be about a 43 millisecond difference between the readings due to the 8,000 or so miles between them that the signal had to travel. Obviously if the transmission was instantaneous like her theory predicted, the difference would be zero. Or, of course, transmission might not work over such a tremendous distance. Probably *won't work at such a distance,* she reminded herself.

To her astonishment it showed a difference of 31 nanoseconds! *Far* less delay than the 43 millisecond delay you would expect with light speed transmission, but not instantaneous either. Her existing theory didn't have room for an intermediate result. She sighed and wondered if there could be a problem with the clocks? They were *supposed* to be far more accurate than that! Could temperature changes or vibrations during the flight have affected them? She pondered a few minutes, then decided that she couldn't think of any way to evaluate the discrepancy.

Oh well, she'd still transmitted from one side of the Earth to the other using only the 5 volt USB power supply from the clock... That was a pretty astonishing accomplishment all by itself. It'd just take more work to determine the actual speed of transmission.

~~~

Ell went upstairs to Dr. Smythe's lab. When she peered in she saw a bearded young man leaning back with his feet up on a desk. He had his head cradled back in his hands, staring up at the ceiling. She gently knocked on the jamb of the open door, but there was no reaction. She knocked a little louder and he sighed. He turned his head to look at her without moving the rest of his body, "Yes?" His tone wasn't exactly surly, but it was obvious he wasn't happy.

"Hi, I'm Ellen Symonds, Dr. Smythe's expecting me?"

He lifted an eyebrow, "Who?"

"Ellen Symonds."

"Are you sure?"

"Sure that I'm Ellen Symonds? Or that he's expecting me?"

The young man just lifted an eyebrow again.

Irritated, Ell said, "Never mind. Allan, please let Dr. Smythe know I'm here at his lab."

The young man dropped his feet to the floor and frowned at her. They stared at each other for a few minutes, then Dr. Smythe came around the corner and walked past Ell into the lab. He looked around a moment inside the lab, then turned back to, Ell. A big grin quirked up at the corner of his mouth. "Oops! You must be Ellen?"

"Yes sir."

"I'll be damned!" His grin got even bigger as he looked her disguise up and down. "Come in! Come in! I've set up some stuff over here." Smythe moved quickly over to a cluttered table along a side wall. "I assume you've met Kevin here?"

"Not by name, but we spoke." She glanced at the young man. His brows were up.

"Kevin Lamont, grad student. Don't let his impenetrable affect fool you, he's actually fairly intelligent." Smythe threw another grin over his shoulder. "Let me see your prototypes."

Ell pulled the pair she'd brought for testing out of her pocket and handed them over. She heard Kevin get up and curiously move over to their side of the lab.

Smythe looked at the prototypes, "Ah, nice! USB 5.0 I assume, powered from the port?"

"Yes sir."

"Very good, very good." He plugged one of the PGRs into a jack on his AI and the other into a small stereo audio-player device. He tilted his head a moment, looking mildly surprised.

Kevin reached out and touched the power switch on the stereo. The sound of Dolby's, "She Blinded Me with Science" throbbed out of it. Kevin said, "Professor, you listen to the damndest stuff!"

Smythe excitedly washed his hands together.

Kevin said, "What is it, some kind of micro transmitter for USB signals? There are quite a few commercial models available..."

Smythe picked up a Faraday cage and dropped it over the stereo. The sound continued. "Can they transmit through a Faraday cage?"

Kevin looked puzzled, "Maybe? If the signal's strong

Smarter

enough or uses a frequency that'll bounce up through the bottom of the cage?"

Smythe grinned, "Metal table, my man, metal table."

Kevin frowned, "Hard to believe it has enough power off USB to force a signal through. Is it using a really short wavelength?"

Smythe winked at Ell, "See, told you he wasn't as dumb as he looks."

Ell grinned back and shrugged, but didn't say anything.

Smythe turned to Kevin, "Well man, let's have some foil to wrap it in and see if we can block those short, short wavelengths."

In a few minutes they had wrapped the Faraday cage in layers of foil, but could still hear the muffled stereo playing.

Kevin said, "What the hell?"

Smythe clapped his hands together, "What the hell indeed! Let's unwrap it."

Shortly they had done their best to detect any electromagnetic radiation emanating from the PGR without success, Smythe exclaiming in delight after each test.

Kevin suggested a few other tests which they carried out.

They also did some tests Smythe had prepared ahead of time. Smythe turned to his student, "Well Kevin, got any more ideas?"

"Take it apart?"

"Nope, not allowed. But you sit here and see if you can figure it out. You're always telling the undergrads how smart you are. Let's see you prove it.

"Elll-en," Smythe said stumbling a little over her new name, "you come with me to my office and we'll talk."

In Smythe's office he beamed at her. "Amazing! *Just* as awesome as you said. Have you tried to determine the speed of transmission yet?"

"Um, it has normal fiberoptic data transmission rates at present. It may be able to be pushed up, but I haven't made any attempts as yet."

"Well that's fantastic. But I was asking, is it light speed?"

"I... I think it should be instantaneous, but I've got conflicting results."

"Really? How?"

"Well I checked out a pair of picosecond accurate clocks and FedEx'ed one to Australia with a PGR attached to its output."

"PGR?"

"That's what I'm calling them, for photon-gluon resonance."

"Oh, great idea! You're not telling me that you transmitted a signal from Australia to here with a device powered on a five volt USB port are you?"

"Um, yeah. According to the equations, distance shouldn't matter. Apparently it doesn't, at least across the diameter of the earth."

"Fantastic! So what's the difference in the readings between the clocks?"

Ell reached into her bag and pulled out the PGR-clock. "At light speed there should be forty plus milliseconds difference. My theory would predict instantaneous transmission, but..." She set the PGR-clock in front of him, "You can see it's reading 31 nanoseconds. Faster than light, but not instantaneous. I'm hoping that there's something wrong with the clocks, but I'll have to wait until it gets shipped back to know for sure."

Smythe looked at the display then got a subtle grin, "Hmmm, Bert?" he mused to his AI, "Show me Hafele and Keating's experiment from back in the 1970s. He looked up at the screens of his AI. "Hah! Just when I thought you were too smart by half, you miss something like this!"

"Like what?" Ell grinned crookedly at him. "Teach me, Yoda."

"Yoda!" He cackled, "'Tis merely *relativity*, my dear Watson. The speed of the flight around the earth in a plane should have resulted in a small amount of time dilation partially offset by lower gravity up where the plane was flying."

Ell smacked her palm on her forehead. "Of course! I bow to your wisdom sensei. I'll try to calculate how much dilation should have occurred."

"Hah, no need grasshopper. Back in 1971, Hafele and Keating sent an atomic clock eastward all the way around the world and it resulted in a 59 nanosecond loss, close enough to double the 31 nanoseconds you got from sending your clock half-way around the world! Transmission *must* be instantaneous or damn close to it! Hah! Amazing!"

They grinned at each other for a few moments, then he said. "I've *got* to know how this works. Can we make a non-disclosure agreement, i.e. that I hereby agree not to reveal the means or mechanisms of your device to anyone, nor to attempt to exploit it for commercial gain in any form, and you tell me how it works? MIT has a standard legal form for non-disclosure that I can have my AI modify to suit our situation. Since the form's written to protect MIT when we disclose our tech to others, you can be pretty sure it is written on the side of protecting you adequately."

"Sure."

He glanced upward, "Bert? Please modify the standard MIT nondisclosure agreement to wit, that 'Ms. Ell Donsaii is revealing to me,' and let her look at it."

A moment later Ell was studying the form on her slate. She looked up, "OK."

"Oh," Smythe shook his head, "I'd advise you to take your time to completely read and fully understand it before you agree. You can take a couple of hours if you want. Meanwhile I can talk to Kevin and do a couple other things."

"Um, sorry, I read very quickly. I do understand and agree. Taking more time won't help me."

Smythe rocked back, "Damn, I keep forgetting that I'm talking to a wunderkind. OK, I agree on my part, though I obviously can't agree for MIT. But I promise to keep it to myself and not even let MIT know anything for now. With our agreement to this contract recorded by both of our AIs, the legal bases should be covered. You can go ahead and explain it to me."

Ell and he spent half an hour going over the design of the device, how it worked and how it fit with her equations. Smythe sat up and said. "That is going to revolutionize the world! First you have to patent, then you have to publish and commercialize. Tell me about your relationship with Johnson and NC State?"

"Well I love the U, but Johnson, not so much." Ell went over her relationship with Johnson and showed Smythe parts of the audio-video clip she'd compiled from her AI record that showed Johnson telling her to stop working on her project and demanding that if she did work on it, it be on her own time and with her own resources. She also showed him their final meeting when Johnson had demanded to be let back in and told him that he was apparently trying to understand her apparatus at present.

Smythe leaned back in his chair, "Amazing! He seems like such a nice guy at the Society meetings." He sat back up, "Well, I agree he shouldn't have rights to any part of your invention, though perhaps the University has a small claim. Why don't you go ahead and submit a patent while you're waiting for their decision, you don't want to take the chance he'll figure it out himself and beat you to a patent. He may be a jerk, but he's a very, very smart jerk. Unfortunately, there's no physical law that ensures that brilliant people are nice."

Ell looked worried, "I hadn't thought about how important it might be to get a patent quickly. I've got a serious problem because currently I'm nearly broke with virtually no collateral for a loan. I can re-up with the Air Force, in fact I have to, if I'm not in grad school. But it'd be quite a while before I got a paycheck. I was hoping that it'd be possible to interest a company in the technology without disclosing the mechanism, and then get *them* to pay for a patent?"

"Normally, that's exactly what I'd advise you to do. However, that could take months to years, and if Johnson submitted a patent before you successfully arranged it, it'd be a serious problem. Would you take me on as an investor?"

"Uh, sure! How would that work?"

"You'd promise me, say 1% of your royalty stream, in return for which I would promise to personally fully fund the patent application process, arrange meetings with industry and advise you on industry negotiations. Essentially, as an interested party, I'd do anything and everything I could think of to make sure you successfully commercialized this product. I'd pay you $100,000 now for that 1% interest, so that you wouldn't be broke. And, so you'd be sure I'm continuing to work to make it happen quickly, $50,000 every six months until you receive more money than that from whatever commercial entity we deal with."

"Surely you'd want more than 1%?!"

He laughed, "Surely I would, but I'd consider myself very, very lucky to get that. I don't think you have any idea how much this is worth. One percent will make me very, very wealthy."

"What if the patent fails, or NCSU beats us to the patent, or something else happens? I don't have collateral for a $100,000 loan."

"It's not a loan. It's an investment. If you lose, I lose. That fact alone guarantees that I'll bust my ass to make it happen and happen quickly so no one beats us to it."

"Wow, that'd be great! Thanks. But, I think we should agree that, in case it doesn't make it big, we should split the income 50-50 until you've gotten double your money back."

Smythe laughed, "OK, but not making it big won't be an issue, I promise. But I agree to such a contract as witnessed by our AIs, do you?"

"Sure."

"Great. Bert," he said to his AI, "contact Aaron Miller, tell them it's an emergency." Smythe turned to Ell, "He's a patent attorney who worked with me on a couple of my own patents. He'll be *great* for this."

Chapter Nine

By the end of the day Ell's head was whirling. Smythe had transferred $100,000 to her and she'd sent $5,000 to her mother. Smythe had demanded to see the patent attorney that day and paid $2,000 to have the attorney cancel his other appointment that afternoon. They were submitting the patent under her Ell Donsaii persona which had meant Ell had to rent a room where she could remove her nose prosthesis and wash off her bronzer, dark mousse and makeup. Smythe waited in her hotel room while she did this, making calls to start arranging corporate meetings. When she came out of the bathroom as "Ell," Smythe looked up with a startled expression. "Forgotten what I looked like?" Ell grinned.

"No, I'd just forgotten how stunning you are. It must be an odd experience having people react to you so differently as Ell versus Ellen, huh?"

Ell flushed. "I don't think I'm all that good looking, but people sure do react differently to the two versions of me. I think that's just because Ell's kind of famous, don't you?"

He laughed, "Sure, that too. But you're quite beautiful. It's hard not to stare when you're in the room. Just slap me if you see me gaping OK?"

Ell laughed. Somehow the honest admission kept his intent gaze from being creepy.

~~~

They went to the patent attorney's office and went over the device with Miller until he understood it pretty well. Then they worked out a patent strategy. Smythe paid the usual patent fees plus an extra $10,000 if Miller had it fully submitted by the close of business the next day. Between meetings they strategized their disclosure to possible existing corporations and to some venture capitalists. On Miller's advice, Smythe hired an attorney named Exeter full time. Exeter specialized in IPOs. He'd arrange and negotiate with possible corporate partners. The next morning Smythe cancelled a class so that they could meet with Miller again, who'd worked on the patent application until late at night. They went over it carefully to make sure it covered all possible uses.

Once they'd electronically submitted the patent, Ell flew back to Raleigh as Ellen Symonds. They'd set a plan to meet with possible corporate partners the week after Thanksgiving.

Since her mother wouldn't be able to send her broken car for Ell, Ell rented a car at the RDU airport. Then she went out shopping for some business clothing to wear at the negotiations to come. She had to take off her "fat pants" in the dressing rooms to try stuff on, and that felt kind of weird. She also bought other new clothes for her Ell Donsaii persona because that version of her hadn't worn much except uniforms for a couple of years now. Then, since it was Friday, she dropped by West 87 before heading back to Morehead City.

When she walked in, none of the gang was there and she wondered if they had some other event that night. She went to the bar and ordered a Coke then went over to watch some of the pool players. "Care for a game?" a low voice rumbled beside her.

Ell looked up. It was Silent Joe! She saw Bill standing, holding a pool cue at a table across the room. Silent slowly winked at her.

Amused that Silent Joe seemed to be the only man who ever noticed her as "Ellen," Ell shrugged and said "OK."

They walked over to a table that Bill had already racked up. Bill lifted a Coke and nodded to her, "Sorry I acted like such an ass the last time we met. I'm an obnoxious drunk and Silent here's making me cut back."

"How do we play with three of us?" Ell asked.

Bill snorted, "Oh, no! You're not going to try to give us that, 'I'm a beginner who doesn't know anything about pool,' crap are you? Remember, *we've* seen you play."

Ell shrugged, "Sorry, I really am a beginner who just happened to get *really* lucky that night. Hasn't that ever happened to anyone else?" She looked up at them innocently.

Bill and Silent looked at each other, then Bill snorted and said "OK, you play cutthroat like this..."

~~~

After the explanation, they played a couple of games, Ell carefully putting in one ball each time her turn came up and losing badly. The two bikers were actually quite good. She bought a round of drinks after each game, but everyone stuck with soda, even Silent, who true to his moniker rarely said anything. Then she saw Jerry across the room, staring wide-eyed at her. She broke off from the pool game and went over to him. "Hey, Jerry. Where's the rest of the gang?"

"You're playing pool with *those* guys?!" he said,

staring across the room at Bill and Silent.

"Um, yeah, they're pretty nice when they haven't been drinking."

"Humpf! Well the rest of the gang's been in Johnson's lab all hours the past couple days, trying to figure out whether you really made your spin bumping experiment work or not."

Ell's forehead wrinkled. "'Spin bumping' never worked. What worked was photon-gluon resonance."

"Yeah, yeah, whatever. They've been trying to get it to work. Thank God *I* never had anything to do with it. The way Johnson's been riding Roger, you'd think that he expected Roger to have watched your every move, day in and day out."

"Ouch, but what about Emma?"

"Johnson remembered you saying something about Emma helping you with a circuit and when he found the two different circuit sets you'd had the fab lab make, he started grilling her about the one she helped you with."

"Oh no!"

"Oh *yes*. He's been yelling nonstop. You'd think it was *their* fault!" He shrugged, "It doesn't sound like they've made much progress though."

Over Jerry's shoulder, Ell saw the front door of the bar open and James come in, followed by Emma and Roger. She went over to them, "Oh man, guys! I am *so* sorry! Jerry told me that you've gotten dragged into this mess between Johnson and me?"

"Dragged kicking and screaming, damn right!" Emma said. "He is *such* an ass. And a hateful man to boot. He isn't even my professor and he's had me down in his lab all day today, working on stuff I know nothing about while my own research is going to hell." Her shoulders slumped. "But, Ellen?"

Smarter

"Yes?"

"He had the fab lab build more copies of your circuits. Both the one you made that was so expensive, and the redesign I helped you with. They *don't* actually do anything! Are you sure you're OK?" Emma looked quizzically at her.

Ell looked at the others and realized they were all looking at her with concern on their faces. She realized they may wonder if she'd gone manic or otherwise deluded herself. "Um, yeah, I'm fine." She didn't want to tell Emma she'd intentionally had her build incomplete circuits. "The circuits need a couple of other components before they function." Which was certainly true, they needed their nanotubes in addition to the two solder bridges. "But it's fine with me if you just tell him you think I was crazy and making crap up."

James said, "Oh believe me, *we've* been telling him *that*. Sorry, but without you there to defend yourself and since you're apparently not ever intending to come back, we've been letting your reputation slide right down into the toilet. Well, not Roger here, he can't seem to stop defending you—don't know what's gotten into him."

Ell looked at Roger who had a sheepish look on his face. He looked down at his feet, then back into her eyes. "Hey, Ellen. I, I just can't stand it when he says... stuff about you."

They sat down. Emma said, "It's true, Roger's been risking life and limb; well at least sanity and eardrums, defending you. To hear him tell it we've been associating with a saint. I'm expecting the Pope to call about your beatification any time."

"Hey thanks," Ell said and winked at Roger. "But you guys just go ahead and disparage my reputation with

Johnson. I'd *prefer* it if he decided that my project was all in my imagination."

"Really?" they chorused.

"Yeah. I'm hoping to be able to commercialize some devices from it, but even though Johnson should have no rights to the tech after telling me to drop it and making me work on it nights and weekends, I don't want to have to *fight* him for the rights."

"Really? But what commercial value would it have? Johnson says you claimed it can be used in communications?"

"Yeah. I think so. Though a lot of work would need to be done to make it viable." Ell thought to herself that it was true. Work would have to be done to *commercialize* it. They would assume that, like most discoveries, it would need an incredible amount of engineering work done to make it into a viable and usable product. Most prototypes were marginally functional, look at the Wright brothers' first airplanes. There was no reason to tell them that the prototypes she'd already made were working great.

"Well, you certainly didn't put enough information in that invention disclosure form for us ordinary humans to figure it out."

"Yeah, the IDFs really don't ask for the details and I didn't think I should put them in before patent protection was underway."

A waitress came and took their orders. Their conversation turned to more pleasant things.

When it came time to go, Roger got up to walk her home again. He took some good natured ribbing from James. "Hey, Rog, you going sweet on this girl? That why you've been defending her to Johnson?"

He just ducked his head and shrugged. Ell realized

that, tall and smart as he was, he was actually pretty shy. *Maybe he doesn't have much more experience with this boy-girl stuff than I do?* She turned to James and said, "Hey, now you back off my knight in shining armor. We damsels need our protection from evil professors and horrid Rigellians."

They all turned and grinned at Jerry. He grinned back and said, "Ah *hah*. It's good to see you're finally beginning to heed my warnings!"

Ell and Roger headed out the door. After they'd walked a block, Roger's hand found Ell's again. They walked in silence a while, then talked about their plans for Thanksgiving. Roger would be heading home to Morehead City. Ell realized there was some chance she might bump into him as "Ell."

This time, when they got back to Ell's apartment complex, Roger walked her up to her apartment door. They turned and faced one another uncertainly. Roger said, "Every time I bring you home lately, I worry it'll be the last time I see you."

Ell crinkled her eyes as she grinned up at him, "Not if I have anything to say about it."

He fumblingly put his arms around her and gave her a hug, leaning his head down next to hers. He felt her lips next to his ear. She quietly said, "Roger?"

Her breath in his ear gave him goose bumps. "Yes?"

"I think we're both kinda geeky and shy?"

He drew his head back and looked into her eyes from a few inches away. He shrugged.

Ell pulled him closer and whispered in his ear, "I just want you to know it's OK if you kiss me."

~~~

Roger's goose bumps were back. "OK," he mumbled,

then slowly moved his lips to hers, startled by the minty taste of her lipstick. *Wow!* He thought to himself, *this is* way *better than I imagined.*

~~~

Ell savored the sensations of her first real kiss, thinking wonderingly about how warm and firm his lips were. It made her feel all warm and fluttery inside and sent pleasant tingles down her spine.

~~~

Roger felt her hand move up his back to rest on his neck and pull him more firmly into the kiss. The feel of her fingers there somehow added to the kiss. Then she broke the kiss and leaned back eyes twinkling. She said, "Hey, I really liked that! Maybe again sometime?" she let go and turned to her door.

Roger resisted the temptation to reach out and pull her to him again. Something about this girl was magical. He didn't want to ruin it. "Me too, and yes, definitely," he said.

She stepped into her apartment and swung the door closed, stopping with it open just enough for him to see one eye, which winked at him before she closed the door the rest of the way. He turned to go home, feeling a mix of frustration and ecstasy.

A bright moon lit his way home through a cool crisp evening.

He didn't have any trouble dodging the Rigellians.

***

The next day Ell washed off her makeup, bronzers and mousse, converting back to her Ell persona. She left her apartment in a hoodie with a scarf over her face and headed down to her rental car, but she didn't encounter anyone during the brief walk.

The drive to Morehead City was uneventful and she parked a block away from her grandmother's house. When she walked up to Gram's house she didn't notice the small camera on the fence, but that was hardly surprising since it was tiny. Its buried electronic brain sent notification to its masters in Goldsboro though. They exclaimed to finally see the young woman they'd been looking for. "Mr. Li," one shouted, "she back in Morehead City!"

He grunted, "Finally! Gather the team, the mission's a go."

~~~

Ell opened the door and called out, "Mom? Gram?"

They were sitting at the dining table studying a slate, but both looked up in delight at her entrance. "Ell!" they said together. Hugs and excited catching up were followed by preparation of juicy BLT's for lunch.

Before taking her second big bite, Ell nodded at the slate they'd been hovering over, "What'cha workin' on there?"

Kristen said, "Trying to analyze our finances. My attorney says that even though he doesn't think the divorce will get me any money from Jake, I *should* get my own money back. But I have to get through till then and the obnoxious SOB's even managed to get a big chunk of my salary sequestered until the divorce's concluded. Not because he really thinks he's entitled to it in the end. Just because he knows how to work the system so he *can* make it hard for me. I think he keeps hoping I'll knuckle under and crawl back to him like I used to."

"Aw, Mom, I am so sorry you ever got hooked up with that creep."

"Me too, kid, me too. Anyway we were trying to make sure we can make it a few more months on Gram's pension and my partial salary. That $5,000 you sent really helped."

Gram said, "I don't want to take a loan out on the house, but I will if we have to."

Ell said, "I don't want to count chickens before they're hatched, but there's a pretty good chance that the device I invented will bring in a fair amount of money."

Gram said, "Well that might be, but we shouldn't count on it."

Ell could tell that her grandmother really didn't think there was *any* chance her little granddaughter could've invented anything that'd bring in a significant amount of money. But that was OK. Ell didn't want to count on the invention either, unless and until she actually had money in hand. With the flights to Boston, she'd burned through almost all of her remaining savings but, other than the $5,000 for her mom, hadn't quite gotten into the hundred thousand from Dr. Smythe yet. She intended to return that hundred thousand to Dr. Smythe if the invention didn't work out. The money he'd spent on the patent was bad enough.

She said, "I've told the Air Force I'm available, but they told me that I'll have to do an abbreviated Officer Training course since I didn't do all four years at the Academy. So I won't actually start until the officer's training starts in late January. I won't get any paychecks until a month after that. However, I do have an investor who's advanced me some money on the invention—we can dip into that if we have to."

"Really?" Her mom said. "Well I guess *someone* must have faith it's going to make money."

***

The next few days leading up to Thanksgiving were lazy and uneventful. Ell spent some time talking over the net to Smythe and Exeter about exactly how they'd present the idea to their potential buyers the next week. Ell drove to Raleigh to get the PGR-clock that had been shipped to Australia and send it back to Australia. They wanted to have the clock in Australia for their demonstration. It was addressed to an international patent associate of Miller's named Allison who'd hold it for the demo.

On Thursday, Ell, her mom and Gram cooked all day for the big dinner they traditionally held with a few of their neighbors each year. Ell found herself sitting next to a little girl who looked up at her and said, "You look a lot like that Olympic gymnast."

"Do you mean Ell Donsaii?"

The little girl nodded thoughtfully, "I think so."

Ell smiled, "That's who I am."

The girl's eyes got big and she said, "Are not!"

Ell grinned at her a moment, then said, "OK, you've got me there. Aren't you Mary Estes from across the street?"

The girl nodded. From across the table, Mrs. Jenkins said, "Ell, could you pass the butter."

As Ell said "Sure." and reached for it, she heard Mary gasp. She looked back down at her.

Eyes open very wide, Mary said "Are too!"

Ell grinned down at her. In a conspiratorial whisper she said, "Would you like to see the medals?"

Mary nodded her head up and down, finger in her mouth.

"After dinner we'll go see them OK?"

Wide eyed, Mary nodded again.

***

On Saturday afternoon Ell, feeling a little stir crazy, went into town to do some Christmas shopping. She didn't notice a van pull out to follow her. On the way home she had a whim and turned into Emmerit's restaurant, it was almost dinner time and she could use something to eat. As soon as she entered, she saw Roger's sister Shelly seating people. She waved hello to her old classmate.

Shelly's eyes widened. She squealed delightedly and hugged Ell at the hostess station. "Ell! It's so great to see you! Are you here to have dinner?"

Ell could feel people staring at her, "Yep. Where should I sit?"

"Are you by yourself?"

Ell nodded.

"Oh, great! Sit here at the counter, we can catch up!" She indicated an empty stool next to the hostess station.

"Sure."

"Etta?" she said, looking up into the screens of her AI. "Call Roger and tell him Ell Donsaii's here in the restaurant."

A little alarmed that her disguise might have been penetrated, Ell said, "Roger?"

Smarter

"My older brother. He just thinks the world of you and made me promise to call him if you ever came in." Conspiratorially she said with some indication of disbelief, "He's a physics grad student so he *says* he admires you because of that paper you wrote, not your gymnastics. That's what he *claims* anyway!" Shelly winked at Ell as if men were entirely too transparent. Her brow furrowed at Ell's look, "I hope you don't mind?"

Ell said, "Not at all," she smiled, "I *love* talking about physics." She took her seat and Shelly took her order personally.

Between pauses for Shelly to seat other customers, Shelly and Ell talked about what'd been happening in the lives of their classmates. A couple of other people that Ell knew came by, and a couple of kids asked for autographs, and then Ell heard a familiar voice, "Ms. Donsaii?"

She turned to see Roger, apparently having come in through the back entrance of the restaurant. She restrained her impulse to jump up and give him a hug. Then she almost used her "Ellen accent." Finally she managed to say, "Yes?" in Ell's normal voice.

"I'm Roger Emmerit, Shelly's brother. I asked my sister to call me if you ever came in so that I could personally tell you how much I admire your paper on quantum physics and the fifth dimension. I've hoped to see you in town for a long time."

"You've *read* it?" Ell managed to put a surprised lilt in her tone.

"Oh yes Ma'am. I'm a physics grad student at NCSU and I just think the implications are amazing, though I do have a little trouble following some of your new math conventions. In fact, there's another grad student in our lab who's been working on testing some of your predictions."

"Really?!" Ell put a surprised and excited tone in her response.

"Yes. She works in the same area that I do. I'd love to work on your stuff myself, but I was already deep in another project when your paper came out."

~~~

Roger stared at Ell. She looked familiar, of course, from all the times he'd seen her in the news. But there was something else, almost as if he knew her somehow. She had perfect, flawless skin with a scattering of tiny freckles. Her cute turned up nose seemed perfect for her face. He realized her eyes were the same intense green as Ellen Symonds', *Maybe that's what makes her seem so familiar?*

Ell said, "Oh, that's great. I've been hoping *someone* was trying to test my predictions. Of course, there's always that niggling concern that whoever does is going to prove me wrong."

"Well I've got good news for you there. Of course, I should let Ellen tell you herself. Can I call her for you?"

Nonplussed at the thought of being connected to talk to herself, Ell quickly said, "No, I'd rather not talk to her myself. It'd be better if she could avoid any semblance of bias by being able to say she doesn't know me. Could you just summarize what she found?"

Roger seemed disappointed that he wouldn't be able to introduce them, but said, "Sure, she worked out a way to use high energy photons in a modification of the double slit experiment while measuring flux in the slits. You may be aware that current flux sensors are much more sensitive than they used to be? In any case there are fluctuations at both slits, suggesting that the single photon goes through both slits just like you predicted!"

Ell made a little fist pump, "That's great! Has she submitted for publication yet?"

Roger looked abashed, "Well, kinda. She and her professor got in a huge fight and she quit the University. He refuses to have his name on her paper. She sent the paper to a journal anyway, but I doubt a journal's going to publish it with him in opposition. It's a real shame because she's absolutely brilliant!" He shook his head. "She has so much to offer physics. I hope she's able to get into grad school somewhere else."

Touched, Ell said, "Brilliant?" It was nice to hear what people really thought of you. At least, it was when they thought nice things.

"Well, not like you, but still pretty amazing! I'd been having trouble with my own study for months and when I was commiserating with her over my problem, she pointed out in an offhand way what I'd been doing wrong. She said it like it was no big deal. And she's only a first year grad student! Though, the problem she saw with my experiment *was* based on your theory. Ellen's a lot more familiar with your theory than I am." He shrugged. "If only," he paused, "she's kind of hard headed! If only she'd just apologized and kowtowed to Dr. Johnson like the rest of us do, she'd still be in grad school."

Ell restrained the impulse to reach out and punch him. "So, was she hard to work with then, hardheaded and all?"

"Oh, no!" Roger leaned conspiratorially to Ell. "Actually I'm crazy about her. She's sweet and a great friend." His face fell, "But I expect she'll move away now, and I don't know if we'll be able to stay in touch."

"You'll just have to try harder then, eh?"

Allan spoke in Ell's ear, "Phil Zabrisk is calling."

Ell put up a finger, "Just a minute Roger. Allan put Phil on... Phil, are you in North Carolina like you said?"

She heard Phil's voice, "Hah! Better than that. I'm in Morehead City. I drove down to surprise you. I dropped by your house and I've been hanging out with your mother and your Gram a bit. Having given up on you returning spontaneously, I'm just leaving your house to come find you. Dinner's on me. Where are you?"

"Um, at Emmerit's." For a moment she was reluctant to have the two men in her life in the same location, but, after all, Roger didn't even *know* he was with Ellen. "It's a restaurant."

"OK, I'll be there in a minute. Save a chair for me."

Roger was looking at her quizzically. "An old friend from the Academy's in town and coming down to visit me here at the restaurant. Um," she turned to Shelley, "could we move to a table?"

"Oh sure." Roger turned to Shelly and they quickly arranged a table for Ell. Shelly was going to put her at a two top, but in a whisper that Ell heard, Roger insisted on a four top, apparently hoping to sit with her a bit longer.

~~~

Roger watched Ell gracefully stand and follow Shelly to the table they'd arranged, carrying her drink. She was wearing a short pleated skirt and low heels.

He had a hard time pulling his eyes away.

Ell turned and said, "Roger? Would you sit with us? I'd love to hear more about your results."

Roger came eagerly over and took a chair. They

resumed talking physics and Roger described his experiment and how much better it was going since "Ellen" had recognized the polarization issue. Ell suddenly realized that another component of his project could be affected by the quantum effects that her math predicted.

In the middle of one of his sentences she again held up a finger, "Wait one, Roger."

~~~

Roger sat admiring her while she stared up into her HUD and talked quietly to her AI a moment. Distractedly she said, "Do you have a slate here?"

"Uh, no. But I can borrow Shelly's."

He got up and brought it over. Roger set the slate on the table and Ell scooted next to him so they could look at it together. He was extraordinarily distracted by her proximity, especially when she unconsciously touched him a couple of times. But she exported a file to his AI and the slate, then deftly pointed out how his experiment was affected by her postulated fifth dimension. He'd been amazed by how quickly "Ellen" had understood the problem with his experiment back at the lab. But Ellen couldn't hold a candle to Donsaii. Ell hadn't even *heard* of his experiment ten minutes ago and was already explaining the ways her complex math predicted the results he'd been getting! He swallowed, mind racing with the implications, eyes staring at the slate. *How could she have figured this out so quickly?!* It was almost as if she already understood his entire research project! Embarrassed to be schooled in his own field of study, he didn't even hear a voice behind him say, "Ell?"

~~~

Phil had entered the restaurant minutes earlier and looked around for Ell, expecting her to see him and leap to her feet. He'd been dismayed to recognize her strawberry blond head bent over a table next to some other guy! They were leaning over something on the table in front of them, talking in low tones.

Damn! Did she have a boyfriend now and she just hadn't told him? Phil cursed himself again for not letting her know how strongly he felt about her when they met in Raleigh the past summer. He walked closer and was appalled to see her put her hand on the other guy's arm. But they were looking at a slate; maybe she was just explaining something? To his delight, when he said her name, she did leap up from her seat and throw her arms around him.

"Phil! Hey it's great to see you!" She kissed him. Though it was only on the cheek, he found himself touching the spot. "Sit, sit, we'll order dinner! They have great seafood here!"

~~~

Roger looked up to see the guy who'd been in the news with Ell. One of her fellow Olympians, the guy was a wrestler. He was also handsome and had a real Greek god physique. Roger felt skinny, drab and inconsequential by comparison. He rose, "Ms. Donsaii, thanks so much. You've helped immensely. I truly, *truly* appreciate your help and the opportunity to meet you. All my friends will be envious!"

~~~

Despite thinking that mixing Roger and Phil would be like mixing oil and water, Ell found she really didn't want Roger to leave. She said, "Oh, it was a lot of fun talking physics. Won't you stay and have dinner with us?"

~~~

Phil, at first relieved to hear the man call her "Ms. Donsaii," implying that they weren't that good a friends, subsequently felt dismayed to hear him get invited to eat with them. Nonetheless, he smiled and said, "Sure, have dinner with us, I'm buying."

~~~

Roger, ecstatic to get to spend more time with Donsaii, said "It's my parents' restaurant. Let *me* buy, I get a discount." He gave them a broad wink.

Shelly showed up with a menu for Phil. She looked up at him, "Are you Phil Zabrisk? From the Olympics with Ell?"

"Um, yeah."

"Oh! I *so* admired you in the Olympics!" She smiled sunnily at him before heading back to her station.

Ell felt a twinge of jealousy. Shelly'd always gone out with the really cute guys in school and Ell had felt a little drab in comparison, even though, rationally she knew her own looks were better than ordinary. *This is silly,* she chided herself, *it's not like Phil's my boyfriend or anything.*

The three of them sat down, but their conversation was clumsy. Ell realized it was because the two men had absolutely nothing in common. She and Roger could talk physics and she and Phil could talk about the Academy, but it was like she was carrying on two separate dialogues rather than all of them contributing to one conversation.

Shelly came back to take their order. After they'd all ordered she asked, "Hey, do you mind if I eat *my* dinner with you guys? I got Brenda to cover the desk for me."

~~~

Roger cocked an eye at his sister, knowing that on a busy Saturday night like this, having the hostess out would cause some problems, but she gave him a pleading glance. Then he realized that Brenda wasn't here yet. Shelly'd actually gotten Brenda to come in on her night off! Shelly must want this pretty bad...

~~~

Ell, taken aback by Shelly's obvious interest in Phil, nonetheless she said, "Sure."

After all she couldn't possibly say no without being rude.

The dinner went pretty well from there. Shelly's bright personality carried the conversation to inconsequential areas and drew them all in, though Shelly spoke more to Phil and therefore Ell spoke more with Roger. When they'd eaten Shelly said, "Hey Jones-Alias are playing at McAllister's, you guys want to go check them out?"

After some hemming and hawing, they all agreed and Shelly shepherded them all out to the dimly lit parking lot, deciding that she should ride with Phil to, "Show him the way." Ell thought about pointing out that Phil's AI could find McAllister's just fine. But she just shrugged and said, "Roger, you want to ride with me?" She felt inordinately pleased when he nodded eagerly.

Ell squeezed next to a white panel van that was parked very close to the driver's side of her car. She'd just thought to herself that someone must have parked manually because an AI wouldn't have parked so close, when the door to the van slid open and hands reached out, one grabbing her arm, the other shoving a Taser into her back. Waves of agony pulsed through body as her legs collapsed.

Being dragged bonelessly into the van she thought to herself, *Not again!*

Chapter Ten

Shelly was watching Ell enviously as she walked gracefully across the parking lot with Roger. Somehow even the simple act of walking appeared to be an act of elegantly perfect coordination when Ell Donsaii did it. Shelly thought it was unfair that Ell was so attractive *and* so accomplished. When she got into the passenger side of a van Shelly was puzzled a moment, then Ell's flaccid movements registered. "Phil! Someone just dragged Ell into a van!"

Phil was already aware. He'd been wondering how he got saddled with Shelly. The pretty brunette was a nice enough girl, but *not* who he'd driven down to Morehead City to meet! Ell's slender legs had had his full attention when they buckled.

Phil found himself running toward the van as its tires spun. It pulled forward rather than back, out across the curb and wildly into traffic. Despite a valiant effort on Phil's part the van quickly outdistanced him.

As he ran back to his car he recited the license number to himself while he had his AI call 911. "There's been a kidnapping! The victim is Ell Donsaii, reddish blond, five foot eight or nine. White van, license number LME-4406, I'm uploading my video file of the attack!"

He jumped into his car, unlocking the doors so Roger could get in. Setting the car to manual he squealed out of the lot in pursuit. "Roger! Where's that road go?"

"The coast!" Roger responded grimly.

~~~

In the back of the van Ell felt the wild takeoff of a vehicle obviously driving with its AI turned off. It rocked wildly and she heard squealing from its tires and the tires of vehicles that were trying to avoid hitting it.

Meanwhile her captors had dumped her on her back and were applying the oh-so-familiar cable ties to her wrists. She began to get muscle control back and tried kicking out. A jolt from the Taser blasted through her again.

By the time her muscles would respond again, her wrists and ankles had been tightly cuffed together. She resolved to wait until she had better muscle control before she tried anything again. They were unplugging her AI and turning it off. She shouted, "Blitz! Apprise Phil."

She was glad to see they trusted the switch she'd jiggered and didn't remove the battery. "Blitz" was the code word she'd set for Allan to report an attack to the police, Chief Bowers, and her family. Then it would continuously update GPS location to them, all without any detectable activity since it'd be sending the information out through the paired PGR unit back on the lab computer system at NCSU.

Ell, getting some motor control back, looked around the van and saw three Asian men in the back with her... and her mother! Damn them! Kristen also wore handcuffs and ankle cuffs with a chain of cable tie loops between her ankles. Duct tape covered Kristen's mouth, but her wide eyes spoke volumes about her state of mind.

The van bumped and swayed wildly to a halt. One of the men slammed the door open and the other two hauled Ell out like a sack of potatoes. They dragged her over and into the back of a SUV. One of the men got in the back with her and the others slammed the back door shut. Ell squirmed around and saw them forcing her mother into the back seat.

Out the front window Ell saw the masts of boats, so they must be in the parking lot of one of the marinas. The driver of the van came over carrying Ell's AI and a box Ell thought must be a net jammer. He got into the driver's seat and they careened out of the parking lot, obviously with the SUV's AI disabled as well.

One of the Asian men sat in the passenger seat, one beside Kristen in the back seat and one sat cross-legged beside Ell in the cargo space. Since Ell could barely see lights out the side windows she assumed the windows of the SUV were heavily tinted.

The man sitting next to Kristen reached up and switched on the dome light, then turned, waved a pistol and said, "You may call me Mr. Li. We do not wish to harm you Ms. Donsaii; we only want to consult your physics expertise. If you cooperate, neither you, nor your mother will be injured." He gestured at Kristen with the gun. Eventually you'll both be returned to your home, none the worse for the wear."

Ell grimly recognized the same 9mm Smith and Wesson type weapon that the Asians had in Boston. She gritted her teeth and nodded jerkily.

The man sitting next to her pulled another Smith and Wesson out of a shoulder holster and nodded meaningfully at her before putting it away. Ell carefully thought back to her previous capture and decided that she was confident she remembered the location of the safety and its safe versus unsafe positions. She wondered to herself whether they'd be carrying them with a round chambered? It'd be difficult to rack the slide with her wrists bound so closely to one another.

Ell wriggled around and sat up, then said quietly, "Mom, you OK?"

Her mother couldn't speak with the duct tape over her mouth, but she nodded spastically as the SUV continued to race down the road. Soon they crossed the bridge onto the Atlantic Beach barrier island.

~~~

Phil's AI said "I have a message from Ell Donsaii's AI."

Phil said "Go!" Then he suspiciously wondered how Ell's AI could be functioning. Surely a kidnapper's first move would be to turn it off?

An AI voice came on, "Mr. Zabrisk, Ms. Donsaii has asked that you be informed that she's been attacked and kidnapped -"

"I know that!" Phil snapped.

"- and that by my GPS she's currently in a vehicle proceeding South on the Atlantic Beach Bridge toward Atlantic Island at an average speed of 50 miles per hour. Her mother and four men of Asian extraction are in the vehicle with her. Do you have any questions?"

"Have you told the police?!"

"Yes. They assure me they're responding."

Suddenly Roger yelled, "There's the van!"

Phil looked where Roger pointed. A white van stood, panel door open, parked crookedly at the marina. He slowed to turn in, then said, "Wait, Ell's AI? Are you sure she's still with you? And why haven't they turned you off?"

"Ms. Donsaii modified the switch on my case so that it doesn't turn off anything but the case lights. Her captors have flipped that switch, but I am still functional. They have unjacked me from her HUD so I no longer have video input. She installed a separate microphone so that I still have audio. I've heard them talking to her, and she has spoken to her mother. In addition, all four of the Asian men are in the vehicle. I can hear them speaking Mandarin Chinese amongst themselves."

Phil pulled back out onto the road and Roger started yelling, "*That's* the van! Where are you going?"

Phil said, "Report the van to the police. Ell's AI is sending me a message that she's in a vehicle on some kind of bridge going south."

"What? How can her AI be functioning? Her captors would have to be idiots! What if they're putting her in a boat at that Marina?"

"I'll explain after you've reported in to the police." Phil said as he sped up.

"Was it Atlantic Beach Bridge? Because that's just up ahead!"

To his AI, Phil said, "Chuck, take over the driving and be sure we follow the route Ell's AI is reporting to you! Emergency override the speed governor on this car and get us going as fast as we can without wrecking!" The car surged ahead, then slowed to turn onto the bridge.

~~~

Ell said, "Mr. Li, where are you taking us?"

"Oh, now, I *can't* tell you that."

"What do you hope to learn from me? I only have a physics theory, not any useful applications." At least Ell hoped they didn't know about PGR and therefore about her Symonds persona or trips to Boston.

"Our leaders believe your theory will lead to many useful applications. They've already employed many researchers who are dedicated to discovering those uses. Now we want you to be able to work with us in state of the art laboratories, developing applications for the benefit all of mankind. We think you'll enjoy the experience and we intend to make it worth your while!"

"Yet you're starting by kidnapping me?"

"We *asked* first! You told us your government wouldn't allow it. We *cannot* allow them to monopolize the technology that comes from your theories."

Ell said, "So, you'd immediately release the results of our research to the world?"

"Well… certainly! Just as soon as it had undergone evaluation to be sure that it would be safe for worldwide release."

Ell felt even more certain that these people were working for a sovereign government, almost certainly China. They were obviously associated with the first group to kidnap her. She couldn't let them take her, or her mother, outside the United States, but she was concerned that they were already making for a boat. If only she could be sure Allan had the word out? Surely the police would take it seriously with Allan sending them the video record of her abduction up to the point he was unjacked? Probably Roger had a video record too, and perhaps Phil or Shelly as well.

On the other hand, waiting for rescue, seemed foolish, the more people working the problem the better.

Ell looked around to consider her resources. Her wrists were bound tightly with interlocked cable ties that didn't have any connecting loops. This resulted in her hands crossing at the wrists. If she dropped into the zone and took the Smith and Wesson out of the shoulder holster of the man beside her, *and* it had a round in the chamber, she would easily be able to shoot all of the men in the car before they could respond.

But she'd have to shoot Li in the head to be sure he didn't injure her mother. Ell didn't want to do that if she could think of *anything* else. And, if there *wasn't* a round in the chamber, she'd be in deep do-do, unable to rack the slide to chamber a bullet in a reasonable period of time.

As Ell racked her brains for another strategy, the car suddenly pulled off the road to the right or inlet side, rolling into a driveway and then under a house on stilts. *Damn, this house probably has a boat! That'd be why they chose it.*

Li turned to Ell and her mother. "We're just going to rest here in this nice beach house for a few days until all the fuss dies down. Mrs. Radford?" He said to Ell's mother. "If I take off your gag, will you stay quiet?"

Kristen nodded.

"This will hurt, but it's best done quickly." he said, then ripped the duct tape off her face. "There now, not so bad eh?"

Kristen shook her head, though her eyes glistened.

"Now, we'll need you to shuffle into the house while we carry your obstreperous daughter, OK?"

Kristen nodded and he leaned over and opened her door. The man from the front seat helped her out and started her up the stairs. The other man met Li at the back of the SUV and opened the gate.

Li said, "I'll check for watchers, wrap her in the carpet."

It turned out that Ell was lying on a piece of carpet,

which they proceeded to roll up around her. When Li came back, they lifted her out and two of them carried her up the stairs. Li came up after them, carrying the net jammer, Ell's AI and a small satchel. They put Ell and Kristen in a back bedroom that had two beds, and then Mr. Li rubbed his hands together, obviously pleased. "Mrs. Radford, We'll make you a sandwich now. Ms. Donsaii, I believe you ate at the restaurant?"

Ell nodded her head, amused by Li's polite concern, then heard the faint sound of a siren. Her heart leapt, but then it sank. *Surely the police wouldn't come into a hostage situation sirens blazing?* It had to be for something else. She saw Li tilt his head, then look up into his AI screens. He said, "The net is jammed correct?" He picked up Ell's AI and looked at it, checking the switches and lights. He tilted his head and smiled, hopefully getting word from his AI that their net jammer was blocking traffic adequately.

~~~

Outside, Phil and Roger had coasted to a stop a hundred feet short of the house where Allan said Ell was located. Allan'd confirmed hearing Ell's voice again and that they'd climbed stairs into a house. The two men ran the last bit on their toes and snuck into the yard. Roger touched Phil on the shoulder and then leaned close, "There's probably a boat in that shed down there. I'm going to go down and disable it in case they're planning to use it to take her somewhere."

Phil nodded, his attention focused on the house itself. There seemed to be a couple of lights on in the back, but not much of the light was filtering out to the front window. An old SUV was parked under the house, certainly big enough to have carried six people here.

Then Phil heard the sirens. *Could it be? Surely not! Not with sirens would they?* An Asian face appeared in the window. Peering East in the direction the sirens came from. Then Phil thought he heard a siren from the other direction. The face jerked back from the window and Phil could hear shouting inside. He moved in under the house where he could lurk in the dark and watch both stairwells, as well as the SUV.

~~~

Upstairs, one of the Asian men came running back and started shouting in what sounded to Ell like Chinese. Li answered tersely, once, twice then shrugged. He turned to the women, "Those sirens *can't* be for us, but just in case we'll go down and wait in the boat. Mrs. Radford, you will go with Hao here," he indicated one of the men. "Ms. Donsaii?" He nodded at the rug.

Ell tensed to resist but Li took out the Taser. "Now, now, be nice." He indicated the rug again and Ell resignedly rolled on to it. Minutes later she was being carried down the back stairs.

~~~

Phil watched a small man run down the back stairs and head out to the boat shed. Shortly, another man came down the stairs leading a shackled woman. Her hair was too long to be Ell's. Next, two more men came down carrying a long rolled bundle. With relief Phil saw the toe of a shoe peeking out of the end of the roll. They all headed toward the dock and boathouse.

Phil followed a little behind and to the right so the bundle, on their right shoulders, would block their view of him. As they were stepping out onto the dock the sirens arrived from both directions and stopped at the front of the house. Apparently the local police *would* arrive at a hostage situation, lights and sirens blazing. Flashing red and blue lights from the front strobed the rear area making Phil feel very visible. The man leading the shackled woman turned to look back and Phil could imagine his eyes widening as he saw Phil.

Phil stutter stepped up onto the dock and shoved the hindmost man off into the water, grabbing the bundle he hoped contained Ell and pushing with it so the second man fell into the water too. He felt the bundle squirm as it fell and heaved to keep it from going in the water, but it still struck the deck pretty hard. The carpet fell open to reveal Ell bound hand and foot.

His heart soared but then something struck his shoulder. Simultaneously he heard the bark of a gun and saw a muzzle flash from where he third man stood by the boathouse. The other woman was down on the deck like any sensible person would be in the middle of a gunfight.

Phil reached down, scooped Ell up and leaped off the dock into the water on the right side of the dock, keeping his eye on the shooter. He saw another muzzle flash and heard the gun's bark, then Phil heard a meaty "thock" and the man flew off the dock into the water on Phil's side. A skinny guy stepped out from behind the man holding an oar in his hand. Phil recognized Roger.

Damn, this water's cold, he thought, clasping Ell to him with his left hand to make sure her head stayed above water. He noted grimly that his right arm seemed weak and his shoulder felt dead. Phil's feet reached the bottom, thank goodness, so he started backing toward shore.

One of the Asian guys pulled himself up on the other side of the dock and started to cross to Phil's side, but then the cops finally showed up. "Hold it right there! Hands up! Now! Behind your head! You too," he said, waving his pistol at the one still in the water.

~~~

Eventually, they fished the man Roger'd cold-cocked out of the water. They removed the fourth one from the boat where he'd still been desperately trying to start a motor from which Roger'd removed the fuel line. An ambulance arrived and took Phil to the hospital. They let Ell ride with him, mostly because they thought she should be checked over too.

~~~

A very nice policeman took Kristen and Roger down to the station to make a report, then drove Kristen home and came in for coffee. Kristen insisted Officer Duncan come in, "To explain everything and help calm Gram's nerves." Gram later confided to Ell that "*My* nerves were fine," but that she'd, "Never seen Kristen looking so darned moony eyed."

~~~

The hospital determined that the bullet had gone through Phil's deltoid muscle.

Though Phil would be very sore for a while and need some rehab, he shouldn't suffer much permanent damage. In a sling, Phil came home with Ell and she slept on the couch so he could have her bed at her Gram's house.

In the morning Ell announced her plan to take her rescuers out to Sunday brunch. Kristen invited Officer Duncan. They all had a nice time and rehashed the events, even having a few chuckles. At one point Officer Duncan, or "Miles" as he preferred to be called said, "You know the damndest thing? Those guys had a fully functional net jammer with them that was running full blast. When we got to the house we lost all comm." He turned to look at Ell, "So, even though your AI was somehow getting the signal out to the police department, saying you guys were down at the dock, the department couldn't tell *us*. We had to find you with the Mark 1 eyeball." He turned to Ell, "Do you have some kind of special military grade AI Lieutenant? Something that could punch a signal through that net jammer?"

"Please call me Ell." Ell said brightly, wondering what to say. "It *is* a military AI and certainly has some special capabilities. I'm not supposed to talk about them though." She felt Phil staring at her and gently kicked his ankle.

Miles shook his head and said, "Well I wish *we'd* had that tech last night, we'd have found you a lot faster."

~~~

After the brunch Ell, Phil and Roger decided to ride back to Raleigh together. They took Phil's larger car with Ell's and Roger's cars following by themselves in platoon. With Phil's arm in a sling Ell sat in the driver's seat on the theory that, in case of computer failure, you'd like a capable driver in that seat.

Phil quizzed Ell about her special military AI that could punch through a net jammer.

Ell managed to fob him off by simply telling him that she'd upgraded hers in response to being kidnapped during the summer. Fortunately, he didn't question the *existence* of an AI with enough transmitter power to be

185 | P a g e

capable of punching through. Otherwise the conversation was pleasant.

Ell very much enjoyed herself, having the two men in her life with her at the same time, but not realizing that she considered each of them to be a kind of undeclared boyfriend. She felt guilty and amused and excited all at once. As they neared Raleigh, Roger said from the back seat, "Ell, I can't wait to tell my friend Ellen that I not only met you, but spent the weekend fighting off kidnappers with you!"

Phil, in the passenger seat, shot Ell a look. He knew Ell, had an "Ellen" alter ego, but not that Roger knew her.

Ell gave him a minute headshake.

Then Phil's eyes widened as he took in the meaning of the statement. Choking he pretended to cough at the realization that Roger was intending to tell Ell as "Ellen" about the weekend they'd just experienced. When he got himself in control, he said in a choked voice, "Her name's Ellen what?"

"Symonds." Roger said dreamily. "She's really nice, smart too."

Phil snorted, "Physics majors!" He started another bout of choked coughing.

Ell glared at him out of the corner of her eye. "Phil, are you going to be OK?" she said, as if she were concerned.

~~~

They dropped Roger off as they passed through Raleigh on the way to the airport. Ell kissed his cheek and hugged him goodbye, "Thank you for saving my life!" she whispered in his ear. He held the cheek she'd kissed as he watched them drive away.

Smarter

~~~

After they dropped Roger off, Phil threw his head back and howled. "So you're working both sides of this guy, Ell-Ellen? I mean I've heard of guys fooling around with *two* women, but never *one* woman fooling around with a guy while disguised as *two* women!" He chortled merrily.

Ell glared at him again. "Perhaps you should take another of your pain pills?"

"Um, No. I'm feeling pretty good right now."

"But, you're about to *start* hurting, just as soon as I start hitting you..." she raised an eyebrow at him.

Phil cowered away from her in mock terror.

Ell said, "Roger's really nice, unlike certain rude and uncouth people I hang out with sometimes!" She chuckled, "Actually, I met him in grad school as Ellen, and only later realized he was from my hometown where I'm Ell. Believe me; it's been a little difficult to keep my roles straight this weekend. But he's just a very good friend of Ellen's; he's not a boyfriend." She mused to herself that she wouldn't mind if he was though. On the other hand, Phil could be pretty nice himself?

Phil looked at her seriously. "Hey, Ell?"

She turned, "Yes?"

"I hope you know just how important you are to me? Actually, I've been feeling kinda jealous of this new Roger guy. I mean, I took a bullet for you and *I've* never gotten a kiss."

"Hah, you've had plenty of pecks on the cheek like he just got, but here's another." She leaned toward his cheek, but Phil turned quickly to capture her lips on his. With Ell's reaction time she could easily have avoided it, but found she didn't want to. She leaned into it, pressing her soft lips to his firm ones, then reaching up to grasp the back of his neck and pull him into it a little harder.

Fred, her "Ellen" AI spoke in her ear. "You have a call from Roger Emmerit."

Ell broke away from Phil's lips a moment to say, "Sorry, can't take a call at present." Then she leaned back to Phil.

Eventually, she broke free from Phil again, leaned back and winked at him, "Hey," she said throatily, "Hope you noticed I didn't kick you in the nuts this time!"

He snorted, but by then she'd leaned in for another kiss.

~~~

For the flight to Boston, Ell snuck into a bathroom and changed back to her Symonds persona. She wanted to minimize her time as Donsaii while the Chinese might still be looking for her. While in that getup, she called the Tech Development Office at NCSU to find out what they had decided to do with her invention. When she reached the same man who had spoken to her before, he leaned back in his chair with a smirk on his face. "Ms. Symonds! I understand you quit your graduate program?"

Ell studied the man, thinking to herself that he was a trivial and mean-natured person. "I resigned, yes. I found Dr. Johnson's treatment of his subordinates, including me, unacceptable."

"Well, I'm sorry *you* couldn't get along." His expression betrayed no concern and his slight emphasis on the "you" made it obvious where he thought the fault lay. "In any case, I just spoke to Dr. Johnson this morning. He's gone through your experimental setup thoroughly and assures us there's no scientific basis for your claim of quantum transmission. The committee met and concurred that the University should not expend any more resources on this idea of yours."

Ell sighed, trying to sound disappointed. "So, I have to patent it by myself?"

"I'm afraid so."

"And the University renounces all rights to it?"

"Well the University will continue to claim five percent of any royalty stream, should you actually be able to commercialize." Patronizingly he said, "However, I'd advise you to speak to your parents or other advisers before attempting a patent. The patent process is exceedingly expensive, whether or not your device actually works or has any value."

Barely able to restrain her expression Ell simply said, "Yes sir, I will. Goodbye." She broke the connection.

Boarding the plane, Ell called Roger. "Sorry I couldn't take your call earlier," she said, using her "Ellen" accent. A spike of guilt went through her over the fact she'd been kissing Phil while refusing Roger's call.

Roger sounded excited, "Hey, no problem. You're not going to believe who I hung out with this weekend!"

"Who?!" Ell hoped her amusement sounded like excitement to him.

"Ell Donsaii! You remember she's from my hometown?"

Ell murmured assent.

"Well she came into my family's restaurant yesterday and my sister called me so I could go down and try to meet her. She's *really* nice! Not only did I get to talk to her a bit, she actually let me have dinner with her and her boyfriend from the Air Force Academy!"

"Wow! That's really cool!" Ell said, while thinking, *Boyfriend?*

"Then when we were leaving the restaurant, some guys kidnapped her!"

"Really?!"

"Yes! Her boyfriend and I chased them to a house on the beach where they apparently intended to take her out to sea. He knocked the kidnappers into the water while they were carrying her rolled up in a carpet. One of the kidnappers actually *shot* her boyfriend!"

"Oh my God! How awful! Are they OK?"

"Yeah she's fine and his wound was just to the muscle. She took us all out to brunch this morning and was really nice to everyone. Even one of the policemen. She's just a *really* sweet person. Oh, and I told her about your research! She was *very* interested."

"Really?"

"Yep, you *really* should call her and talk to her about what you found on *both* your studies. I told her just a little about my project and she immediately made some great suggestions. I can't wait to try them out. She's just... phenomenal!"

"Hey, what am I, the consolation prize?"

"Oh no, you're brilliant too... but I don't think *anyone's* in Donsaii's class. She's... one of a kind."

Simultaneously complimented and mildly put down, Ell snickered at herself for the bemusement percolating up through her brain. "Well OK. Hey, I'm going to be out of town for a few days, but should be back by Friday. Maybe I can get by to hang out with you guys at West 87 Friday night?"

"Great! See you then."

Chapter Eleven

Ell spent the flight musing over her romantic life. She'd spent most of her teenage years without a single amorous connection, first because of her shyness and youth in high school, then because of the rules at the Academy. Now she had two at least somewhat romantic relationships. Almost three, if you counted the relationships between Roger and Ellen and between Roger and Ell more than once.

She wondered if she should feel guilty that she seemed to have a borderline boyfriend-girlfriend relationship with both Phil *and* Roger? But, she thought, she loved the fun she'd had with both of them and neither had spoken to her about committed or monogamous relationships. The kissing had been very nice too! *Different with each, but thrilling with both,* she mused, rubbing her lips gently.

She decided she'd just do her best to enjoy this part of life, a part of life that most kids had a *lot* more experience with by the time they reached her age.

***

Back in Boston, Ell met with Smythe and their two attorneys, Miller and Exeter. Miller had investigated the Air Force's rights to any invention by Ell and determined that, since she'd been detached when she'd made the invention, they'd be able to claim royalty free use of the invention, but none of the royalty stream.

The patent had been submitted, both in the US and worldwide. Though it'd be months to years before the patent would be approved, they'd established priority and could define the invention as patent pending.

Exeter had incorporated "PGR Tech" and had arranged a meeting the next day with seven large companies or venture capital groups, all of whom were bound by non-disclosure agreements.

All that the companies knew so far was that they were being offered an opportunity to examine and bid on a new communications technology that didn't depend on wired, fiberoptic or radio connectivity. They didn't know who the tech had been invented by, though Dr. Smythe's name had been liberally used to entice them, so at present they probably assumed he'd invented it.

The companies had been instructed to bring whatever test equipment they might need in order to be able to evaluate PGR Tech's claims as well as their own data files to transmit in order to confirm transmission and accuracy.

Ell only had the six pairs of prototypes, one original and five of the newer smaller ones. One pair connected to Australia and another to the lab computer at NCSU to provide an unbreakable link to the net for Ell's AI, so there were only four PGR pairs available for evaluation tomorrow. Therefore four of the groups would evaluate the technology in the morning and three in the afternoon; each of the groups closely watched by one of the four of them. They carefully discussed how the prototypes should never leave their sight.

Bidding would be the morning following the testing and would follow an auction format.

Ell said, "I'd like to go look at the rooms we'll be using and retest the prototypes. Also, I want whatever information we have on the groups that are bidding. I assume that I have the right to reject groups at auction?"

Exeter said, "Well sure, but why would you reject a group? Surely we want to accept the best offer?"

Eyes flashing, Ell said, "A group of Asians, probably associated with the Chinese government, has kidnapped me *two* times in the past six months! If I sniff anything *suggesting* those SOBs might be bidding, I do *not* want them to have access."

Exeter swallowed at the transformation of the usually pleasant young woman's demeanor from mild mannered to frightening. "Oh well, then you may want to cancel Lenovo's invitation. They're a Chinese corporation—though they do have very deep pockets."

Ell's eyes narrowed, "Lenovo!" she hissed, blatantly displaying her dislike. "What I'd like to do is show it to them, then tell them that they can't have it."

"What reason would we give, if they're the high bidder?"

"That the inventor doesn't like them?" She sighed and leaned back. "Actually, I don't know that Lenovo was actually involved, just that the kidnappers used the Lenovo name to entice me the first time. But, I *do not* want a Chinese corporation to have access, so please uninvite them."

***

The next morning Ell appeared at the hotel with her hair moussed dark but, instead of her "Ellen" spiky do, it was plastered down to her head. She was wearing a tight sports bra, a man's white shirt, loose around the waist and men's Levi's. No "fat pants." Her hourglass figure was practically invisible and her look quite androgynous. She wore pale makeup and brown contacts. Smythe, Miller and Exeter didn't recognize her when she walked in.

Exeter, looking up, said, "Excuse me. This room's reserved for a confidential meeting?"

Ell said with her best English accent, "I believe I'm invited?"

"Oh, whom do you represent?"

"The inventor."

"Huh, Oh! Ell?"

"Yup, I've decided I don't want them to know who I am. I'd like to be here though. Can you guys call me Terry? It seems suitably androgynous."

"But, I thought you were giving the initial introduction to the tech before they break up to eval it in the separate rooms?"

"I'm still up for that."

~~~

When the potential buyers had all arrived and taken chairs, Exeter introduced Ell as "Terry," an expert on the technology. Ell stepped to the front of the room and began to speak. "Good morning. We're presenting you the opportunity to purchase exclusive rights to a new communications technology. Today we'll tell you about its capabilities and allow you to verify them. Tomorrow you'll have the opportunity to bid for purchase of the rights to the tech in an auction format."

Smarter

She reached in her pocket and pulled out two of the PGR prototypes. Holding them up she said, "These are functional prototypes constructed in a fab lab. We estimate that commercially constructed devices could be reduced in size by a factor of at least ten and constructed in quantity for a cost below five dollars each. They are capable of transmitting data from one PGR to the other, and back, at rates similar to current fiber optic data channels, but without the fiber or any other physical connection."

A condescending young blond man in the front row tsked, "So, is this just some new way to multiplex a cell signal so that it provides high data rates? Because, if it is, I have to tell you we have something like that in development ourselves. We wouldn't want to listen to any more of your presentation for fear that when we release our new system you might claim we pirated the idea from your presentation."

"No, as the solicitation stated, and as you will be allowed to test, it does not use radio."

"Laser then?"

"No." Ell stared at him, clearly waiting for him to interrupt again.

"Inductance or something? What's its range?"

"Thank you for asking, we have a small demonstration." She had her AI open a window on the big screen at the front of the room. The screen was divided, one side blank, the other showing an image of a redheaded man standing before a desk, "Mr. Allison?"

"Yes?"

"Please state your location."

"Uh, 410 West Hay Street."

"Hay Street where?"

"Uh, Perth."

"Country?" Ell felt like she was pulling teeth, perhaps she should have told him exactly what she wanted before the presentation.

"Australia."

"You are an officer of Jones and Allison, patent Attorneys in Perth?"

"Yes."

"And you are being captured by two video cameras, correct?"

"Uh, yes."

"And the signal from one's being sent in the standard fashion over the net?"

"Yes."

"And what's being done with the signal from the other camera?"

"Um, nothing, the output cord from it's in my hand." He held his hand up with the end of a white cord in it.

"What's on the desk in front of you?"

"One of the two devices you FedExed to us and had me open this evening." He gestured at a small object isolated on the plain table in front of him.

"Thank you Mr. Allison. I realize that it is late there in Australia and we appreciate you coming in in the evening for this call. Do you know what the device is?"

"Uh, no."

"And have you done any investigation of it?"

"No."

"Is it connected to anything?"

"No." he said, nudging it so that it slid across the table, thus demonstrating that it was unattached.

"Please plug it in to the output of the second video camera, sir."

He picked up the PGR, fumbled with it and the cable a moment. Another video image of him, from a slightly different angle, appeared on the left side of the video screen behind Ell as he took his hand away showing the PGR plugged into the jack. "There you go." He said quizzically.

"And how much power is being supplied to the device?"

"Uh, whatever is usually delivered over a USB 5.0 cable? I think it's 5 volts?"

Ell turned to the room, "Gentlemen and Ladies, the PGR device he's jacked into his camera is sending a video signal from Australia, using only a 5-volt power source, to this PGR here," she pointed to the paired PGR device, plugged into a USB 5.0 cable on the table behind her.

I'm sure you can think of ways that it might instead be sending an RF signal to the net, then over the net to our screen here. So, though it will be difficult to prove to your satisfaction that that is not the case, we have asked Mr. Allison to have several cans of various sizes available. Mr. Allison, could you drop the PGR unit into one of your small cans and put the lid on it now."

He did so but the video image wasn't disturbed.

Ell said, "And now wrap, can and all, in the copper foil."

The man turned and picked up a sheet of copper foil, then wrapped it around the can and wire. The video image remained completely stable.

The blond man in the front row had his arms crossed over his chest. He snorted, "That *cannot* be possible, but I can think of a lot of different ways to fake it."

Ell smiled at him and said, "So can I. If you like, you can redemonstrate this phenomenon with your own representative in Australia, once you've completed your local testing this afternoon." She turned back to the screen, "Mr. Allison. Can you tell us what the other device in the FedEx package was?"

He reached behind him and picked something up off a small table. He peered at it. "It's labeled 'Bensen Atomic Clock.' Below that it says 'picosecond accurate.'"

Ell turned back to the room, "That clock is a pair to this one." She held it up. "They were synchronized prior to shipping that one to Australia." She turned back to the screen, "Mr. Allison, please unplug the PGR from the video cable and plug it into the clock output." Ell picked up a PGR that'd lain plugged into a cable on a side table to this point. The left video image behind Ell disappeared when she did, though Allison was still unwrapping the foil on the right screen. She plugged her PGR into the clock and held the clock up so they could see its display counting hours, minutes, seconds and blurs of numbers in the frames to the right of the "seconds" frame. On screen Allison plugged the PGR into his clock. When he did, a display below the time appeared on Ell's clock, saying "-29ns." Ell looked out over the room, "There is a 29 nanosecond difference in these previously synchronized clocks. That is much less than the 40 millisecond light-speed delay between here and Australia—*if* you could transmit light directly through the center of the Earth. The 29 nanosecond difference results from a relativity induced time dilation as the Australian clock was shipped around the earth on a FedEx jetliner."

The blond man said, "Oh come on! Are you trying to claim transmission is instantaneous?!"

"Yes." Ell said, pausing a moment to look him directly in the eyes. "It is."

"That's *not* possible! I can't believe you called us in

here to witness petty chicanery!"

Ell smiled pleasantly at him. "You are, of course, free to leave. We are, however, demonstrating *facts*. Facts which you will be able to check for yourself later this morning. I would suggest that, if you have factors available to your company in Perth, you ask them to proceed to Jones and Allison, 410 West Hay Street so that they can verify what you've witnessed on the video. Becoming completely confident of our claim of instantaneous transmission might need to wait until you can send one member of a pair of your own clocks to Australia.

"Next, let me tell you a little more about the devices. They use quantum entangled molecules to transmit signals instantaneously from one molecule to the other using phenomena predicted by the equations Donsaii published in Nature last year. The signal travels from one entangled molecule to the other through the 5th dimension she postulated. The power required is only to excite the molecules; transmission does not require any energy.

"Distance between PGRs, as predicted by the equations, does not matter.

"Data transmission cannot be interfered with, short of destroying one of the two PGRs.

"Data rates are essentially the same as fiberoptic transmission, but likely with significantly higher reliability because repeater stations aren't required for long distance transmission.

"Because they depend on an entangled pair of molecules, each device is wedded to another as a pair.

"Transmissions *cannot* be intercepted by any other device, so data encryption's not necessary.

"In short, tomorrow you will have the opportunity to

bid on a low cost technology, offering instantaneous, fault free, high rate, uninterceptable data transmission across apparently unlimited distances without infrastructure."

Stunned silence greeted this statement. Several of the people in the room looked at each other with raised eyebrows, then the blond man said, "But they can only communicate with one another, like walkie talkies? Not like our current net structure where you can connect to anyone? That's kind of limiting."

Ell raised an eyebrow, then spoke patiently, "They are *not* a broadcast media. Neither is the phone function in your AI. A company commercializing this technology would presumably establish switching centers that would take in signals via one PGR pair and reroute them to another PGR that was paired with whomever the caller wanted to communicate. Current phone and data transmissions are routed in just such a fashion. Thus, you could connect to the net at optical data rates, much higher than current radio based cell transmission—from anywhere, to anywhere, without worrying about getting too far from a cell. The cost of such a system would be *enormously* reduced over cellular systems due to the lack of need for transmission infrastructure. It would also be more reliable and *instantly* worldwide. Undersea cables would no longer need to be laid at great cost, nor fiberoptic trunks, nor wire or fiberoptic connections to households, nor cell towers, nor wireless routers."

The people in the room appeared somewhat stunned and glanced at one another again.

Ell continued, "Allow me to point out a few other uses for this tech.

"People, companies, banks and military services who

want completely uninterruptible, uninterceptable, undetectable communications could use direct PGR pairs for communication that did *not* pass through anyone else's switching centers. Banks and unmanned military vehicles, at the very least, would want such communication links.

"Current control of satellites and remote manipulators on the moon, to say nothing of the robotic equipment on Mars, suffers tremendously from light speed transmission delays. If we had instantaneous transmission via PGR, a great deal of work could be done by telemanipulation. Surgery currently can be done in remote areas by remote manipulation, but is troubled by transmission delays and reliability in these life threatening situations. PGR can resolve those difficulties.

"Systems that depend on extremely exact clock coordination, such as GPS could be significantly improved by being PGR connected to the NIST atomic clock.

"The Navy could communicate at high rates with its submarines even while they're deep underwater…" she paused.

"I'll take questions now."

Another stunned silence followed as the people in the room tried to grasp the magnitude of the changes that would result from the simple little device lying on the table before them. The room suddenly broke into excited conversations with multiple hands going up to pose questions. Ell coolly and calmly answered all of their questions except for ones about when they could speak to the inventor.

~~~

Ell, Smythe and the two attorneys spent the day carefully watching while the potential investors subjected the prototype PGRs to every test they could think of, including a number of tests for which the investors sent people out to purchase equipment.

It was, as expected, impossible to keep Ell's name a secret because none of the companies would be willing to invest without looking at the patent application, which of course had her name on it. They had to be able to see the claims of the patent and compare them to existing technology to be sure that they would have a lock on devices made with PGR. Of course, with the PGR principle being described for the first time in that patent, no one else *could* have a preexisting patent on the technology, but they needed to evaluate the quality of the patent claim to determine how likely it would be that a competitor could "work around" the submission Miller'd made.

When they found out that the patent belonged to Ell Donsaii there were exclamations by those who couldn't believe that someone that young could have developed this intellectual property by herself. They demanded to see the audio-video record of the release of all but 5% of the technology by NCSU. Several of the investors demanded a meeting with "Ms. Donsaii" but when asked "what purpose it would serve?" they relented. The important thing, after all, was the working technology and the patent that protected it.

That evening Smythe took Ell out to dinner with Miller and Exeter. There they discussed strategies for the auction the next day and whether to let the Liqx Venture Capital group bid at all after McIntyre, the irritating blond man who worked for Liqx, had tried to leave with one of the PGR prototypes in his pocket.

They decided to require a minimum 10% royalty stream, significantly more than the typical 5-8%, and to require an initial buy-in deposit with the same amount due each year until the 10% royalty was greater than that annual minimum.

Ell asked about the annual minimum, wondering why not just go with the royalty alone?

Exeter said, "We want them to be motivated to develop the technology as quickly as they can. If they didn't have a minimum annual fee, they could take their time while the 20-year time course of your patent's running out."

After a little more discussion, Smythe raised his glass to Ell. "To the only bona fide genius I've ever had the privilege to know personally."

Miller and Exeter raised theirs too, "Hear, hear."

Ell blushed, "Hey guys, I just got lucky. I'm as amazed as you that this actually works. What I really appreciate is your help doing this part. I surely don't have the business skills or connections to have made this happen without you!"

~~~

That night as Ell was getting ready for bed in her motel room her "Allan" AI said, "You have a call from Roger Emmerit."

"Put him on… Hi Roger!" she said, carefully remembering to use her Donsaii accent.

"Hello Ms. Donsaii. I'm just calling to thank you for the insights you offered on my research Saturday night. You were absolutely right! The data I've been getting *does* fit your equations. After struggling with this for ages, I'm finally able to make sense of my results and start writing it up for my PhD! I'm going to have trouble because my advisor, Dr. Johnson, is so sure your equations are wrong. But, I'll wear him down eventually and get it published. And I have you to thank for it. I just can't express my gratitude sufficiently."

"Uh, Roger, I thought we were friends?"

"Wha... I, uh, hope so too?"

"Why are you calling me Ms. Donsaii then? *I'm* younger than you are."

"Well, uh, because of your brilliance! I've got to demonstrate my respect! The way you immediately recognized what I was doing wrong was... just unbelievable."

"Well, I think you'll eventually come to understand me when I say that it really wasn't all that fast," she said enigmatically. "But, anyway, I'm hoping you'll call me Ell?"

"Sure! Ell! But, again, thanks for your help."

"Roger, you probably saved my life there on Emerald Isle, I'm pretty sure I'm still in your debt, but I'm glad I could help."

After they hung up, Ell climbed under the sheets, thinking about Roger and how much she liked him. Then her "Fred" AI came on, "Ms. Symonds, you have a call from Roger Emmerit."

Amused, Ell put on her New York, Ellen, accent and said, "Put him on... Hi Roger."

"Ellen! My experiment's working!"

"Really?"

"Yeah. The results I've been getting all along actually fit, *if* I use Donsaii's equations to run predictions instead of classical theory. It's amazing! I told you I explained my research to her when I met her Saturday and she immediately took a slate and worked out how my problems might be coming from failing to take her fifth dimension into account?"

Fighting to keep from giggling, Ell said, "Yes?"

"She's right! It is *so* hard to believe she's only eighteen!"

"Are you going all moony eyed over this teenager?" Ell tried to say with a dangerous tone, "I thought *we* had something going."

"Oh, Ellen, I *respect* her. I *like* you!"

Ell put a threatening tone in her voice, "You don't *respect* me?"

"Women!" he laughed, "You're just trying to drive me crazy aren't you!? There's nothing I could say that'd make you happy, is there?"

Ell chuckled, "Oh, Roger! Relax, I was just busting your chops a little is all."

There was a long pause, Ell started to worry that his feelings really were hurt, but then he said, "There! Took me a bit, but I've relocated my chops. Hey, did you ever call Donsaii yourself?"

"Well... we've been... communicating, but I can't tell you about it yet."

"Really? Why not?"

"You'll find out soon enough." She said mysteriously. "Night, night Roger."

***

The next morning the Liqx issue solved itself when McIntyre showed up with a new group of investors he'd assembled overnight. He'd separated from Liqx and his new group wanted permission to bid on the tech too. As "Terry," Ell fixed him with a baleful eye, "So you're telling me that your new investors trust you *so* completely that they're willing to invest in this technology without knowing *anything* about it, just on your say so that it has value?"

"Oh no! I thoroughly explained its capabilities to them. Among this group I've assembled are people very experienced with bringing major new products like this to market. Here's a brochure regarding what we have to offer in terms of expertise, experience and backing."

"Does the brochure discuss honesty?"

"Huh?"

"You signed a nondisclosure agreement yesterday, specifically stating that you would disclose *absolutely nothing* about this technology, to *anyone*, without our approval. That was for a minimum period of three years."

"Oh! Well, sure. But I *only* disclosed it in order to bring you this tremendous opportunity!"

"Sorry, we will not deal with someone we can't trust. We won't be accepting bids from your new group. Nor from Liqx unless they agree that you won't be returning to their employ."

McIntyre reddened, stepped close and seethed, "Terry, you have *no* idea who you're dealing with, do you?"

Ell gave him an innocent look and shook her head with an enigmatic smile.

"You're going to regret this! I'll make absolutely certain that Ms. Donsaii finds out that *you* blew a great opportunity. Even if *she* doesn't care, I have the resources to make your life miserable. You, personally," he hissed, "will be ruined in the venture capital world."

Laughing inside, Ell wondered if he really thought she'd back down. To his face, she smiled pleasantly and said, "OKaaay… Now, if you wouldn't mind excusing the rest of us?"

Once Ell had ushered McIntyre out, she had Exeter talk to Liqx to make sure that McIntyre would not be returning to their employ. Once they agreed to that, they were allowed to bid.

Exeter opened the auction by telling the group about the minimum 10% royalty and that they would be bidding on the annual minimum with the first annual payment due within a week of the end of bidding. An older gentleman interrupted, "See here, I can see that you folks don't have much experience with these types of technology commercializations. Ten percent is *much* higher than usual. In addition, it'll be extremely costly to bring this to market, so our company would bear huge risks. It's never agreed to terms like the ones you are proposing.

Exeter grinned. "Mr. Alexander, your company has never had an *opportunity* like this before, and almost certainly never will again. You may not meet our minimum terms, and I suppose it's possible that none of your competitors will either. If so we'll pursue other investors. We're confident that there are companies forward thinking enough to make such a commitment."

Exeter looked around the room and smiled, "Now does anyone wish to start the bidding?"

All six groups had a hand up. The bidding was frenzied initially but then slowed as the representatives in the room reached ceiling limits their companies had set. They began having to call their companies or major investors for authorization to bid higher. Eventually companies began asking for more time to bring in funding partners.

The bidding took almost all day, but by the end of the bidding they'd all agreed to the 10% minimum and eventually Liqx and Hyperion, one of the other venture capital groups pooled their resources for a winning bid of 12% with an annual minimum of 2.1 billion dollars. Rather than the requested full annual payment within a week, they negotiated a transfer of 210 million that afternoon, with the remainder to be transferred within a month. Certain guarantees had been made on the part of PGR Tech, including anonymous access to the inventor as well as the opportunity to consult with "Terry" as an expert in the technology. Finally, there would be a 10% decrease in the amounts owed if, upon testing with their own clocks, the transmissions didn't turn out to be instantaneous.

The company reps left and the crackling tension gradually dissipated from the room. Ell, astonished at the outcome, tried to thank Smythe, Miller and Exeter. Smythe grinned at her and said, "You *do* realize that you're now paying me 21 million dollars a year? I'm forwarding one million of that to each of these guys," he said, indicating Miller and Exeter, "as long as they accomplish certain goals. So, each of us has our own distinct joy in your success!"

Chapter Twelve

Thursday morning, Ell caught a flight back to Raleigh, head swimming when she considered the state of her poor little bank account. It'd so long been on the edge of poverty but now had a balance of almost 208 *million* dollars. Part way through the flight she thought to herself, *I could have flown first class!*

She'd always wondered what life was like up in the front cabin.

She spent the flight wondering what to do next. She needed to tell NCSU and the Air Force about the device, and its patent, and the income from it. Her Ellen Symonds identity would be blown when she told NCSU about their share of the income so she should think about establishing another valid identity if the Marshall's office would help her do it. She needed to tell her mother and grandmother the good news. Which came first? *How* would she tell some of them?

She contacted Gloria at the Marshall's office who told her to come on in. She said they routinely established newer identities for witnesses who'd had their secret identity compromised so she'd be happy to help.

Ell told Allan to contact the Chancellor's office at NCSU.

"Chancellor's Office, Mindy speaking, how may I help you Ms. Donsaii?"

"I'm hoping to make an appointment today or tomorrow to talk to the Chancellor about making a donation to NCSU?"

"Well, as you can imagine, she's very busy. What organization are you representing?"

"Not an organization, just myself."

"Oh, well, *I* can arrange to accept a donation for the University. In fact we can simply arrange an electronic transfer. No need to come in, or to meet with the Chancellor."

"Ah, well, that'd be a problem. I would want to speak with the Chancellor in person before transferring any funds."

"How much of a donation would you be talking about?"

"Mmm," Ell decided to start with 5% of the 210 million that had already been delivered, "ten and a half million right now. Perhaps more, later."

"Oh my goodness, Ms. Donsaii! The stories that I saw on the net didn't intimate that you were wealthy! Let me see here... the Chancellor has an opening tomorrow at three-thirty, would that be satisfactory?"

Ell didn't elaborate on the source of the money. "That'll be fine; I'll come to the Chancellor's office. I'm hoping that you can arrange for Dr. Albert Johnson and Mr. Wayne Stillman to attend as well? They also work at the University."

"I'm fairly sure I can," she said brightly.

~~~

Thursday afternoon, Roger's AI said, "Call from Ellen Symonds."

"Put her on... Ellen! I thought you'd disappeared! Where are you?"

Ell's heart leaped at the excitement in his voice. "I'm in Raleigh tonight. Can I buy you dinner?"

"No! You're broke with no visible means of support. I'm buying! How about if I take you to Mitch's Tavern?"

Ell grinned to herself at the thought that someone who was living on a grad student's salary might by dinner for her when she had 208 million dollars in her bank account. She said, "Sure, seven?"

~~~

Ell put on her "Ellen" persona and arrived at Mitch's a few minutes early, wondering if Roger would've invited some of the other physics grads, or was it just going to be the two of them?

"Ellen!" she heard Roger's voice calling from the back and saw him waving. Ell was pleased to see that he was alone in the booth. He got up and met her part way across the room to give her a hug, "How are things?" He waited for her to sit and then slid in beside her, rather than across.

That gave her a warm feeling too.

"I'm doing pretty well. How's the write up of your research going?"

Roger launched into an excited description of his results, finishing with, "Johnson's being a real prick about it though. He absolutely refuses to believe that my results fit Donsaii's equations. He spends all his time trying to fit them to classical theory and making me redo my setup and rerun the tests to see if we can get a different result."

"Really?" Ell furrowed her brow, "Johnson can be hard to get along with? Are you sure?" Ell grinned at him. The waitress arrived then, Roger ordered the gumbo and "Ellen" the Reuben.

Roger asked, "What're you doing now? Have you gotten into grad school somewhere else?"

"No," she scrunched her face, "I've been trying to see if I can find someone to help me develop my device."

"Oh!" he said, concern on his face. "That must be rough. Are you trying to make applications while you're doing that?"

Ell felt a mixture of relief and disappointment that he hadn't asked whether she'd had any success with selling her device. She hadn't wanted to tell him about her success yet but hoped he'd ask. She shrugged, "Not yet."

Roger looked down at the table. He rubbed at a spot on the surface and quietly said, "I'm hoping that you'll apply at UNC so you'll be close enough that we could still hang out together sometimes."

Somehow, this simple statement really touched Ell. She started to reply, but had a frog in her throat. She put a hand on his arm and, when he looked at her managed to hoarsely choke out, "That's a *great* idea."

~~~

Roger found that the simple touch of Ellen's hand on his arm raised goose bumps. For a moment he wondered dazedly at just how much the girl meant to him. He desperately pondered what to say next, but was saved by the arrival of their food.

He watched in his usual state of disbelief as she inhaled her sandwich.

They spoke of inconsequential matters for the remainder of their meal. Then Ell tried to pay for their meal, but found that Roger had already put it on his credit. *Oh well, it'll probably be the last time anyway,* she thought to herself. She turned and punched him lightly on the arm, "Hey, *I* wanted to buy *you* dinner!

You went and paid already!"

Roger grinned at her. "Just tryin' to take care of my impoverished friend."

On the walk to Ell's apartment Roger's hand found hers again and the walk in the brisk evening air passed mostly in companionable silence. He delivered her to her door again, but this time she immediately unlocked the door and stepped inside. Roger stood uncertainly on the threshold. She turned, "Hey, aren't you going to come in? You're letting all my warm air out!" Ell grinned at him.

Roger stepped in, looking around. Furnished in "student poor" everything in the room clashed with something else. Yet, overall, it looked kind of homey. It was a tiny one room apartment with the bed in one corner and a kitchenette in the other. Ell stood in front of the open frig. "I bought a six-pack of that awful dark beer you like, want one?"

Roger grinned at her, "You trying to get me drunk and take advantage of me?"

She tilted her head a moment, then said, "Yeah, I just can't do without those kisses you've been giving me." She shrugged, "And, I know I've got to get a beer in you to loosen your inhibitions."

He soon found himself drinking a beer on one side of her little table, while she drank a coke on the other. After they'd talked a little more, he looked around the room again. "Wondering how I'm going to make my move when there isn't a couch to sit on?" Ellen asked.

Roger had actually been wondering how he was going to make his move, but with relief he said, "Uh, yeah. Since you don't have a couch, I'm feeling pretty safe."

Ell raised an eyebrow, then said, "Well then, back to

business, I want to show you an idea I had about your research, come look at this." She walked over to her little desk, pulled out the chair and indicated he should sit in front of the screen. She sat next to him on the corner of her bed and leaned on his chair as she pulled up diagram after diagram of his research.

To his astonishment, she already seemed to fully understand what Donsaii'd told him about his project. She began amplifying on it with elegant little observations as he became more and more excited. "Holy crap, Ellen! This is amazing!" he turned toward her and found her face right next to his. She leaned forward a bit. Her lips met his with an electric sensation. Her hand ascended to the back of his neck and a gentle caress made the hair on the side of his head prickle. She started pulling without breaking the kiss and he found himself slipping off his chair and onto the bed with her, all the while still locked in the kiss she'd started minutes ago.

Finally she let go and took a deep breath, "Hah! I'll bet you didn't see that coming, did you!" She grinned crookedly up at him.

"No... but it was wonderful."

"Which? The idea about your research, or the kiss?"

"Uhhh, both!"

"*That's* the right answer." Ell pulled him down for another kiss.

Roger put his hand on her delightfully firm waist and then slid it slowly down onto her surprisingly soft hip.

~~~

Ell stiffened as his hand slid off of her and onto the silicone padding of her fat pants where she couldn't feel it anymore. *Crap*, she thought to herself, *gotta stop this before he realizes I'm made of rubber!* "Uh, Roger?"

Roger had felt her stiffen and realized immediately he'd gone somewhere she didn't want him to go. *Damn it!* He thought to himself, lifting his hand off of her. *I'm rushing it! I thought this was what she wanted, but I should have let her keep leading. I don't want to blow this now!* "Yeah, sorry. I wasn't sure what you were ready for."

"Well, some ways I'm really ready. Other ways... Not so much!" She grinned up at him. "Will you be patient with me?"

"Absolutely. Just as patient as you want."

She leaned up to kiss him again.

After a bit he found himself in her doorway again, zipping up his coat, then starting the walk home, half ecstatic at the time they'd spent together and half heartbroken to be leaving.

***

Ell spent Friday morning with Gloria Sanchez at the Marshall's office, working on several disguises and establishing another verifiable identity. She found herself thinking about wanting to resume grad school. When Gloria was done with her, Ell found herself with hours on her hands before the meeting with the Chancellor, so with her disguise still on she dropped by the testing center and took the Graduate Record Exam in her new identity as Raquel Blandon. She was getting pretty hungry so she rushed through the test to be sure she'd have time to grab a bite to eat before her meeting. When she finished the proctor's head snapped up. He stared at her, then back at his screen. "Excuse me Ms. Blandon, I need to re-identify you."

"Sure, why?" Ell said, anxiously hoping her new identity hadn't already been compromised.

"Uh, you just achieved a perfect score on the math section while spending less time on that section than anyone who's ever taken it at this center. Don't know about other places. But whenever we get really high scores we have to recheck identity to be sure shills haven't taken the test for the student. If you'll just run your finger over the print scanner we'll send it to the national database?"

Ell sighed in relief. Allan should have already notified the national database of her location and that she was using the "Blandon" identity. Sure enough, it reported back that she was indeed "Raquel Blandon."

~~~

Ell grabbed a burger at Five Guys on the way home, then showered and changed back into "Ell Donsaii." *Thank goodness it's cold;* she thought, pulling her big black coat back on. Before she went out the door she pulled the hood up over her reddish hair.

~~~

Johnson and Stillman sat uncomfortably in the Chancellor's small conference room. "Do you know what this is about?" Stillman asked quietly.

Johnson just shook his head. "Mindy said we were meeting with Ell Donsaii, the gymnast that won all the gold medals and escaped from the terrorists. It has to do with a gift to the University, but I have no idea why you or I would be here?" He shook his head. "We've been doing some research on a paper she wrote, but it hasn't been going well. I can't believe it has anything to do with that."

"Wasn't Symonds, that grad student from your lab who claimed to have invented something, supposed to be working on stuff based on Donsaii's theory?"

"Yeah, but how would Donsaii have heard about that? And it wouldn't have anything to do with a donation to the University anyway."

The door opened and Mindy let in a slender young reddish-blond woman. When Donsaii turned toward them they were startled to see how young she looked. She wore black slacks over long slender legs and a simple grey jacket over a cream blouse with a pearl necklace. She had a stunning yet simple elegance. Johnson stepped over, thinking she seemed somehow familiar, probably from seeing her at the Olympics, "Hello, Ms. Donsaii, I'm Al Johnson from the University Physics department," he turned, "and this is Wayne Stillman from the Technology Development Office."

Without speaking, Donsaii shook both their hands, then another door opened and the Chancellor stepped in. She stepped over and said, "Hello, Ms. Donsaii, I'm Chancellor Overhart. It appears you've already met Dr. Johnson and Mr. Stillman?"

"Yes Ma'am." she said very politely. "Thank you for meeting with me."

"Oh, well, we're always pleased to meet with someone of your stature." the chancellor said graciously, also thinking that Ell looked unbelievably young to be so famous. "How can we help you?"

Dr. Johnson interrupted, "I for one, am pleased to have the opportunity to meet you, not because of your status as an Olympian, but because of the paper you wrote on 'Quantum Entanglement through an Unperceived Dimension.' It's certainly stirred up the world of physics."

Donsaii flashed Johnson an enigmatic smile, then turned back to the Chancellor. "It's more a matter of how we can help each other, Ma'am. But I have to give you a bit of background first. May we sit?"

Once everyone had taken a chair, Ell said, "This summer when I graduated from the Academy—"

Stillman said, "You graduated? I thought you were a rising sophomore at the Olympics two summers ago?"

"Yes, well, I completed all the requirements for graduation in two years so they let me go early."

"Oh." The other three people in the room looked at her musingly.

"But this summer I was kidnapped by a group, probably associated with the Chinese government. They wanted me to work on quantum physics for them."

Eyes widened around the room and the Chancellor said, "My goodness! How were you rescued?"

"Well that's a long story, perhaps for another time, but the important thing was that it was suspected they would make more attempts, and in fact they have."

"That's terrible! Do you have guards or something?"

"No Ma'am. The witness protection program fitted me with a disguise so that I could hide from the Chinese."

The Chancellor said, "Oh."

A cold clammy sensation came over Johnson as he suddenly looked hard at Donsaii.

"So I entered your graduate program in physics using an alias."

Chancellor Overhart looked over at Dr. Johnson. His gaze was fiercely focused on Donsaii's face. "An alias?"

"Yes Ma'am, I worked in Dr. Johnson's lab though, unfortunately, we didn't get along."

"You!" Johnson exclaimed. "Are you trying to buy your way back into the program with some kind of donation?"

Donsaii turned to fix him with a gaze like a laser. Then calmly she said, "No."

The Chancellor interrupted, "You recognize her AI? She worked with you?"

"Yes," he ground out, "Though I wouldn't have recognized her without hearing she'd been in disguise. She was enrolled as Ellen Symonds on the recommendation of a friend of mine without even taking the GRE exam. To my *great* regret. She was uppity, difficult and could not stay on task. She kept wanting to work on some crazy theories put forth by Donsaii..." His train of thought derailed as he suddenly realized that he was accusing her of wanting to work on her own theories.

Ell spoke into the awkward silence, "As I said, Dr. Johnson and I did not get along. But on nights and weekends I worked on my own project and it eventually bore fruit in the form of a quantum device useful for telecommunications."

"Not that again!" Johnson exclaimed. He turned to the Chancellor, "I reviewed her notes and reconstructed her devices, they *do not* work. I'm sorry you've had to waste your time on this, Chancellor." He started to rise.

Ell slid a PGR unit across the table to him. "Here's a working prototype Dr. Johnson." She said pleasantly. "Because photon-gluon resonance or PGR units work through quantum entanglement they come in pairs. You'll find the pair to that device plugged into the back of your lab server. You'll find it works very well, that pair saved my life when I was kidnapped again last Saturday. In fact, they work well enough that a venture capital firm purchased rights to the technology."

Johnson stared at the PGR like it was a snake. Chancellor Overhart said, "Is all this true, Al?" He didn't respond. She looked at Stillman and realized he was also gaping wide eyed at the small device on the table. She turned back to Ell, who alone appeared calm. "Ms. Donsaii, this is all very dramatic, but I assume you have a point?"

Ell calmly said, "Yes Ma'am. I reported the invention to Mr. Stillman in the Office of Technology Transfer. He accepted Dr. Johnson's assessment that it was vaporware and so the University refused to assist me in commercialization of the devices. The University did claim 5% of any royalty stream that might eventuate if I were able to commercialize it myself."

"Wait, you're saying you showed Mr. Stillman a working model and he didn't believe his own eyes, or, didn't you have a working model?"

"Um, no, I did *have* a working model, but Mr. Stillman didn't ask to see it or attempt to assess the invention in any way beyond asking Dr. Johnson about it."

"And you never showed a working model to Dr. Johnson either?"

"No Ma'am. At first Dr. Johnson refused to allow me to work on this experiment and then when I was successful, while working on it on my own time, I tried to tell him about it, but he refused to listen during any of my attempts to discuss it." She took a deep breath, "After I'd reported it as an invention he did demand that I tell him about it, but at that point I had succeeded in building functioning prototypes and could not bear the thought of working in his lab any longer. I also didn't want to disclose how they functioned to anyone who might want to undermine my IP. At that point I'd already determined that I was leaving the University."

"But, working under his supervision he would have some claim to the IP."

"No Ma'am. My AI has just sent yours a file of my life while working in Dr. Johnson's lab. Not only recordings of all the times he told me to stop working on this project and refused to assist me with it, but a record of every hour of my every day—in order to document that I, in fact, never worked on this project except on my own time. There were some periods when I worked on it during the day, such as when I had my discussion with Mr. Stillman, but I worked on Johnson approved projects during the night hours prior, in order to compensate for any daylight hours spent on my project. I've reviewed this with my legal advisors and they assure me that Dr. Johnson, having no participation whatsoever in the development of this IP, has no claim on it. They also assure me that the University has, at best, a weak claim to any part of this IP since I worked on it only on my own time and using *my own* funds, even though I did work on it in the University labs and did use some University equipment."

"Oh, *really*?" the Chancellor said in mildly unpleasant tone, but then she paused for a moment, took a deep breath and said, "Before we get our underwear in a bundle about who owns what, how much have you sold this technology for? It may not be worth the lawyer fees to argue over it. Mindy said something about 10.5 million, can that be right?"

"Ten and a half million would be NCSU's 5% share of the first payment I've received, which was..."

"Five percent? So you sold it for... two hundred ten million?!?!"

221 | P a g e

"That was the initial payment."

"Initial?"

"Yes."

"How much total?!" the Chancellor asked weakly.

"I don't know what the total will be. The annual minimum is two point one billion dollars."

A dead silence descended on the room. Johnson sagged back in his chair. The Chancellor noticed that Stillman had started profusely sweating.

The Chancellor cleared her throat, "And you're arguing that the University has no claim?"

Ell calmly said, "My legal advisors say that it would be extremely difficult for the University to *enforce* a claim. However, it is my intent to deliver 5% to the University anyway."

Another pause followed during which the Chancellor calculated to herself that that 5% amounted to 105 million dollars a year. "I... see. And we are meeting today because?"

"Well, because of several things. First, the patent is in my real name, not as Ellen Symonds. I've submitted a scientific paper on PGR, also in my real name. So I could have just assumed that you might not ever realize who Ellen Symonds really was or realize that she *might* owe you money. However, that wouldn't be honest, and when the paper and the product became public, you might wonder about the PGR that Ellen reported.

"Second, until the Chinese stop trying to kidnap me, I would obviously like to keep the fact that I use a disguise a secret. So, selfishly, I wanted to meet with the three of you and reach an agreement wherein you three kept the Ellen Symonds part of this a secret. In return I would agree to donate money to the university, rather than it being a royalty which might lead to awkward questions. I would also like some control of how the money is spent."

"You're attaching strings?"

"Yes, four strings. The first is that if 'Ellen' leaks from *here*, it all goes away. Second, at least 50% of the money shall be spent on Physics, from research, to scholarships, to equipment. The other 50% is to be spent on general university needs and construction, including the construction of any new physics buildings or facilities. Third, any Physics research projects to be funded by this donation would need to submit a one-page summary to me for approval. And, fourth, if I hear of abusive treatment, such as the yelling and belittling of students that Dr. Johnson regularly engages in, I will have the right to cancel that professor's funding from this bequest."

The Chancellor looked sharply at Johnson. "Abusive?"

Johnson interjected, "Just like anyone else, I get frustrated by incompetence and sometimes blow off a little steam. That's not abuse, though some of these young people expect to be coddled *even* when they've screwed up!"

Ell had turned her head to focus on Johnson during this statement, now she tracked back to the Chancellor eyes flashing. "You have the audio video recordings of my interactions with Dr. Johnson. I posit that those interactions, where necessary, could have been handled in a polite fashion with similar, if not better results. I further submit that I am *not* incompetent and performed at *least* up to a level that might be expected of *any* first year grad student. If you disagree, please let me know."

Johnson, purpling during this, exploded, "This is

ridiculous! *I* know how to deal with grad students. There's no way a jumped up undergraduate like her has any right to judge the merits of research submitted by our professors!"

The Chancellor tiredly said, "Al, you don't have to apply for her funding, you can continue to apply to the NSF."

"While everyone else is getting easy funding from her?" He waved his hand in dismissal," Ah well, she'd never fund *my* research anyway."

Ell looked back at him, "Ah, but that's where you're wrong Dr. Johnson. I'd be happy to fund your research. You are comprehensively knowledgeable and insightfully brilliant. You *do* need counseling in interpersonal relations, but I would love to free you up from the need to constantly spend time applying for funding—so that you can actually focus on your research."

Johnson looked at the Chancellor. "We deserve more than 5%, aren't you going to fight for it?"

Chancellor Overhart stared at Johnson for a moment. "First Al, I'm not sure we have a good claim. Second," she looked at Stillman measuringly, "we *said* we only wanted 5%, it would be hard to retroactively claim more. Third, this 5% is a *lot* of money. Fourth, the girl has an income of 2.1 billion dollars a year. That's considerably larger than our entire budget and, if she wanted to, she could probably spend almost all of it just to tie us up in court. If we set our lance to tilt at windmills, we should choose windmills where we have some small chance of triumph."

They stared at one another a bit longer, then Johnson's shoulders slumped. The discussion went on for a while, but they agreed to keep Ell's secret and accept her donation, strings and all.

~~~

Ell put her big coat back on and went back to her apartment, checking a couple of times for tails. She changed out of her dress clothes and into some snug new jeans that she'd purchased on her shopping trip. A turtleneck, little denim jacket, the pearls and her new boots finished her outfit. She headed to West 87, even though it was a little early. She didn't have anything else to do and she felt like letting off steam after talking to Johnson and the Chancellor.

Ell walked in, hung up her big coat and looked around the room to see if any of her friends were there. She didn't see any of the physics grad students so she sat down in their usual booth, ordered a Coke and started thinking about interstellar communications using PGR. Nothing in her equations forbade communications over interstellar distances using photon-gluon resonance of entangled particles. However, you'd have to get one member of an entangled particle pair from one star to another before you could do it. At current travel rates, just getting it there could take thousands of years! You could send an entangled photon from one star to another *at* the speed of light, which would only take four years to the nearest star, Alpha Centauri, but would take a *lot* longer to get to some of the stars that might have earth-like planets.

Even if you succeeded in sending an entangled photon, Ell's equations didn't predict a means for communication using a particle like a photon. She wondered if there might be some way to open a portal from one location to another through her postulated

5th dimension. Perhaps one just big enough to send a few macromolecules through?

Deep in thought, Ell almost didn't notice when someone paused at the booth. She looked up just in time to see Al and Emma turning to go to the next booth. At first, she felt hurt that they'd spurned her, not even saying "hello," then she recalled that she was there as "Ell" not as "Ellen" and they didn't know her. She almost called out, but then sat back to wait some more.

Ten minutes later, again deep in thought, she felt another shadow fall over her table. She looked up to see Roger standing there, looking down at her in astonishment.

Ell grinned up at him and made a little wave, "Hi Roger."

Roger exclaimed, "Ell! What are you doing here?"

She winked, "Ellen told me you come here every Friday night. I was in town and thought I'd drop by and see what all the excitement's about."

Suddenly, Roger noticed Al and Emma in the next booth. "Hey guys, did you notice who's sitting in our regular booth?" They looked up with curious expressions. "Ell Donsaii! Didn't you even look into the booth?"

"Really?" They chorused as they slid out of their benches. "We just saw there was someone sitting there. I guess we didn't look very hard."

Soon they were being excitedly introduced to Ell by Roger. "You know she's from my hometown? I met her last weekend, but my sister's known her since high school."

Ell grinned up at him. "I came down here to meet you guys, sit, sit. Did Roger tell you he saved my life last

Saturday night?"

Roger slid in next to Ell and the others slid in across, "I really didn't. I just whacked a guy on the head with an oar. Her boyfriend from the Academy was the big hero. He got *shot*!"

Ell said, "He's a friendly boy, not my boyfriend, and you took just as many chances as he did, even if you didn't get shot. I owe you both, big time."

~~~

Emma and Al looked at Ell, thinking how young she looked to have accomplished so much. Emma felt a little envy over her flawless skin. Both she and Al were a little thunderstruck to be in the presence of someone so well known in so many circles. Emma leaned forward, and said, "I feel really corny asking this, but my little cousin will kill me if I don't get your autograph?"

Ell smiled, "I'd be delighted, got anything for me to write it on?"

"I'll get a coaster," Emma said, getting up.

A chorus of, "Get one for me too." followed Emma away from the table.

Al asked, "What are you doing in West 87?"

"Well, from Ellen, I knew you guys hang out here and, since I was in town..."

Roger interjected excitedly, "So Ellen finally called you and told you about her project?"

Ell grinned crookedly, "Something like that."

Emma came back with a stack of coasters and a pen. For a few minutes they were all busy calling out dedications for autographs until everyone had what they wanted.

Roger'd just asked, "So what did you think of Ellen's research?!" when Jerry and James came around the corner.

Jerry exclaimed, "Have you heard the news?" Without waiting for a reply, he said, "My service just flagged an announcement that Donsaii's patenting a communication device based on photon-gluon resonance! What the hell! She's going to beat Ellen to it!"

Dead silence descended on the table as everyone sitting in the booth suddenly turned to look at Ell. Jerry noticed the stranger for the first time, then recognized her.

Ell lifted a hand and waved weakly, "Hi." she said.

Jerry simply stared for a moment, then he slowly slid into the booth next to Emma as he said, "Holy crap! What are *you* doing here? Uh, excuse me, pleased to meet you, Ms. Donsaii. But, *holy crap*, what are *you* doing here?"

Ell grinned, "Pleased to meet you too, Jerry. James, please sit down."

James, standing thunderstruck, shook himself and said, "Thank you." He slid into the booth beside Roger.

The waitress arrived then, and after Ell announced that, "Drinks are on me," they busied themselves ordering.

As the waitress walked away, Jerry turned back to Ell and frowned, "How'd you know our names?" he waved toward James.

Ell looked at him a moment, then said, "Now that's an interesting story that has to do with our friend Ellen."

James said, "I don't know if you know this, but she built a device based on photon-gluon resonance too. She's been trying to patent it and she might not be your friend anymore if you've just beaten her to the patent."

Ell said, "Hmm, I've got a lot of explaining to do, have you got a few minutes?"

Nods went around and Ell said, "First of all, I'm not sure if you know that when they kidnapped me this past weekend, that was the second time?" There were some surprised looks at that, though some evidently already knew it by the nods they gave. "The first time was last summer, when I was applying for a spot as a grad student at another school. I escaped unharmed that time too, but the people who've kidnapped me both times appeared to be working for China. As such they probably have the resources to try as many times as they need to in order to eventually capture me. In any case, after they captured me the first time, I decided the safest course was to hide from them under a new, disguised identity."

Roger felt prickles down his back as he drew back to look at Ell, but it was Emma who tumbled to the facts first. "You let them disguise you with a *huge* ass???" she exclaimed.

Everyone at the table stared at her now, trying to reconcile what Emma had implied with what they saw before them.

Emma said, "And that awful nose?!"

Ell looked at her, struggling to keep a straight face. "What is your friend Ellen going to think when she hears what you're implying about her?"

Emma suddenly looked appalled, thinking she'd gotten it all wrong, but then she saw the smirk struggling to surface on Ell's face. "You little bitch!" she grinned. "First you lie to me for a half a year about who you are, then you try to make me feel bad?!"

Ell grinned right back. In her "Ellen" accent she said, "Well *you* did say I had a big ass and ugly nose!"

"Can't believe I was talking to Donsaii the whole time!" and other similar exclamations of disbelief were heard around the table.

Emma exasperatedly said, "All those mornings when I felt so good because you couldn't keep up with me on our runs! You probably could have run me into the ground!"

"Oh no! I have terrible endurance, you were killing me! Besides I was wearing those heavy fat pants, they'd even slow down a good runner."

James said, "Oh my God! I guess it's no wonder that the brand new grad student understood that damned Donsaii math backwards and forward! She invented the crazy stuff!"

Only Roger hadn't said anything so far. He'd been staring at Ell, trying to reconcile the young woman sitting next to him with the woman he'd spent most of a semester becoming friends with. The friend he'd begun to think of as girlfriend material. With embarrassment he realized, the woman whom he'd thought would jump at the chance to call him her boyfriend, but whom he now thought of as far too beautiful and brilliant to consider him for that station. Then Roger's mind rattled around the fact that he'd already spent some time kissing this stunning creature and *she'd* known who she was then—might she actually consider him to *be* boyfriend material?

As everyone else intently discussed this revelation with one another, Ell looked shyly up at Roger and said, "Rog? You OK?"

"Huh? Oh yeah! Sure. Why?"

"'Cause, you're sitting there with your mouth hanging open and you haven't said a word. I hope we're still friends?"

"Oh, yeah! Of course."

"Better than just friends?"

"Damn! You must have thought I was an idiot when I came up to you in the restaurant and started talking to you about physics! And, yes, *always* better than just friends."

Ell put her hand on his arm, "You, coming up to me in Emmerit's, was one of the sweetest experiences I've ever had."

"Yeah sure, right up there with winning those gold medals." Roger smiled at her.

"Right up there. Yes. The best part was when you told me about your friend Ellen, and how much you cared about her."

"Oh…"

"And you told me she was brilliant and sweet and a great friend. It so warmed my heart to find out how you *really* felt about me."

Suddenly James leaned forward, "Ell, do you know if Johnson knows about this yet?"

"Yeah… I told him this afternoon."

"Oooo. I would have loved to be there for that. How…" he frowned, "why'd you tell him?"

"Well, that's something I need to talk to all of you guys about." She paused and when the table had fallen silent, she said, "I told him and the Chancellor and the tech transfer office because NCSU gets some of the money from the commercialization of PGR which I wanted to start delivering, and I wanted them to promise…"

"What!" Emma interjected, "Why do *they* get part of it? You were forced to do it all on your own time! And with your own money!"

"Well I used some of NCSU's equipment and did the

research in University facilities, and to be honest, though I don't like Johnson, he did give me the experimental know how to do the research that discovered PGR. Anyway, I wanted them to promise to keep my use of a secret identity under wraps so as not to give the Chinese clues about how to look for me. Now I'm hoping you guys'll help me keep that same secret for a few years?"

"I'm not sure I'd trust Johnson to keep that promise."

"Hmm, well, there's quite a bit of money involved."

"Really? I mean transmission over entangled particles is pretty cool but, what can PGR do that we can't already do? I mean our data transmission systems work great already."

Ell looked up at the ceiling and recited, "FTL transmission of data at optical rates without a fiberoptic infrastructure or final radio cell networks. It'll be far cheaper, can reach anywhere, and is uninterruptible, uninterceptable and undetectable. Al, remember how you said the radiotelescopes hadn't picked up significant radio transmission from any of the exoplanets?"

"Um, yeah…" he said, puzzled by this apparent non sequitur.

"I think that's because the intelligent aliens out there have all moved on to something *better* than radio."

"Holy crap!" he exclaimed, his eyes glazing while he considered the ramifications.

"Anyway, I'm hoping that you guys'll keep my secret for me?"

There was a chorus of "sure," and "of course."

"Thanks gang."

James sat up, "Hey! I'm suddenly worried that you *let* me win at foosball?"

Ell drew back, "Oh, no. I *wouldn't* do that!"

"Do you swear, upon your friendship to all of us?"

Ell looked stricken, "Well maybe I sandbagged a little?"

"Oh my God! You've *got* to play me one time, full on, no holding back. I'll want to tell my grandkids about it!"

To Ell's surprise, everyone seemed to think this was a great idea and they all started getting up and shuffling over to an empty foosball table. She sat a moment, wondering what to do, then slowly slid out to follow them.

When she got to the table James had already credited it and received an allotment of balls. When she stepped up across from him he said, "Now, I know you're quicker than any human has a right to be. I saw you in the Olympics, remember. I want you to promise me you'll play as hard as you can? I want to show my buddies what *that's* like!"

Ell studied him a minute, then said, "No, I won't play full on for you to 'show your buddies.' You can show your grandkids maybe, but not before then, OK? This girl needs to have some secrets from the world. Maybe not from her friends here, but from the world, yes, *secrets*."

James paused a moment, realized that she was asking for something very important to her, then sighed, "OK, not before I have grandkids."

Ell stepped up to the table, gripped the goalie rod handles on her side and said, "OK, who's going to be my partner?"

James said, "No, no partner, just you."

Ell shrugged and rolled the men on the front two bars up out of the way, and then waited for James to drop a ball in.

When the ball rolled in, Ell didn't try to catch it with her front players, she simply waited for James to move it up to his front men. When he'd stabilized the ball there, he looked up at Ell and saw her focused intently on the ball. Her goalies weren't in very good position. He made a feint to drive the ball to the left, actually drove it to the right and slammed it into her goal.

Except the ball never reached her goal. Ell had let herself drift a little ways into the zone. When James' swung, she moved her nearest man over in front of him, deflecting the ball precisely back to his left where her other man was waiting to drive it the length of the table. In the view of her friends, Ell's men simply appeared to blur. They heard a loud "thock" as her second man hit the ball and a "whir" as the ball flew the length of the table to crash into the back of James' goal. The ball was moving so fast that most of the little group watching had no idea what'd happened. The loud "thwap" the ball made hitting the back of James' goal caused people in the bar to turn their heads curiously. James, simply paused, stunned, then shook his head and said, "Thanks, I've seen enough." and turned to head back to the booth.

As they walked back Emma said curiously, "What just happened there?"

Jerry just shook his head and said, "I'm not sure I want to know."

Ell slid into the booth across from James who was staring into space and said, "You OK?" Inside she cursed herself for actually playing that shot, full on like he'd asked.

James shivered his shoulders, then grinned at her, "I asked, you delivered. Thanks! You really could run the table at pool every time if you wanted to couldn't you?"

Ell shrugged, but didn't answer. The rest of the group sat down and a more normal conversation gradually came to pass.

~~~

A good time was had by all and eventually they broke up to head home. Ell was pleased to find herself walking home with Roger, though after waiting for him for a block, she found she had to slip her hand into his. They walked comfortably along for a while, and then she stepped closer, sliding her arm around his back to grip his waist. She felt pleased when his hand went around her shoulder.

Back at her tiny apartment, she pulled Roger inside, got one of his dark beers out of her fridge and sat on the edge of her bed holding it out to him.

He sat next to her, twisting the cap off, then paused to look at it a moment. "You're not really old enough to buy this are you?"

Ell shook her head and raised an eyebrow at him.

He grinned, took a sip and said, "Ahh, illegal beer, somehow it tastes so much better than legal beer."

She raised her face to his, "You owe me a kiss for the procurement of that fine contraband beverage."

He paid his debt.

Saturday, Ell opened her Gram's door and said, "Hello?"

She was dismayed to see Gram and Kristen sitting at the dining table, looking like they were at a funeral. A man sat there with them, Ell recognized Officer Duncan from the night of her rescue. "What's the matter?"

Kristen sniffed, "As usual, Jake's the matter. The SOB has filed inquiries with the credit bureaus that have ruined both my credit *and* Gram's. We can't even take out loans. My lawyer's throwing in the towel. He doesn't think he'll get paid and doesn't want to piss Jake off because Jake has so much power in local legal circles. Miles here," she indicated Officer Duncan, "has volunteered to loan me some money, but I feel terrible about taking it." She sniffed again, then pulled her shoulders up from their slump. "But enough of my troubles, I'll get through this eventually. How are things for you?"

Ell held up a finger a moment while she mumbled to Allan, then she looked up and said, "Things are going great! Not just for me, but for you and Gram too."

Kristen's brows drew together in confusion. "What do you mean?"

"Commercialization of my invention has been more successful than I ever dreamed."

"Wonderful! Will you get some money soon?"

"Already got some. Check your account."

"But Ell, I need thousands…" She looked up at her AI screens, "Oh my… my goodness!" she put a hand on her chest. "Oh Ell! But that's way too much! You can't give me *all* your money."

Ell sat down beside Kristen and put her arms around her, then leaned near her ear and said quietly, "They're giving me *ridiculous* amounts of money. What I put in your account is just a smidgen. Love you Mom."

Epilogue

Ell leaned back in the lounge chair and listened to the sounds of Bob Marley's "No Woman, No Cry" drifting up from the pool deck below. She sipped her virgin piña colada and watched the young man working his way up the rock climbing wall affixed to the smokestack of their cruise ship. The sun came in at an angle that perfectly lit the play of the strong strappy muscles beneath the skin of his back.

From the next chair Kristen said, "Hey, I see you staring at that young man. Aren't Phil and Roger enough for you? How many boyfriends do you need?"

"Friendly boys, Mom. Not boyfriends. Not yet anyway. Hey, I'm only eighteen, I've only been kissed a couple of times, I've never been on a real date and I'm on a cruise ship in the Caribbean. I think I should be allowed to window shop a little before I commit, don't you? Besides, who knows where the Air Force is going to send me next month? Phil and Roger may both be married before I return to spinsterhood!"

Kristen laughed. "You know that's just what your Gram suggested I should do before I settled down with your Dad."

Gram raised her piña colada, "Hear, hear. You go girl. Window shop all you want!"

Ell turned and gave her mother a look. "Besides, I'm pretty sure you're looking at him too. Isn't Miles enough for you?" She arched an eyebrow.

Kristen sniffed, "My interest is purely that of your chaperone, looking to the fitness of your prospects." She wrinkled her nose, "That one does look pretty good." She winked as she held out her glass.

Ell clinked hers against it.

The End

Hope you liked the book!

Try the next in the series,
Lieutenant (an Ell Donsaii story #3)

To find other books by the author try
Laury.Dahners.com/stories.html

Author's Afterword

This is a comment on the "science" in this science fiction novel. I've always been partial to science fiction that posed a "what if" question. Not everything in the story has to be scientifically possible, but you suspend your disbelief regarding one or two things that aren't thought to be possible. Then you ask, what if something (such as faster than light travel) were possible, how might that change our world? Each of the Ell Donsaii stories asks at least one such question.

"Smarter" asks, what if some genius actually worked

out a way to understand the incredibly weird world of quantum mechanics? If you've never pondered the double slit experiment, you should. It's guaranteed to make you cross-eyed. Then there's the phenomenon of quantum entanglement where entangled particles that are physically separated by long distances have some properties that make them seem to still be in contact with one another. Although entangled particles react instantaneously (faster than light) across this apparent connection, it's not thought to be possible to send information this way—but what if it was?! What if the reason these particles act like they're still connected is because they actually *are*, just through another dimension we can't perceive? Then, maybe we could send information through that dimension!

If it were possible, it'd be very difficult to work out how to do, it but the benefits of figuring it out would be huge!

Acknowledgements

I would like to acknowledge the editing and advice of Gail Gilman, Elene Trull and Nora Dahners, each of whom significantly improved this story.

19862435R00133

Made in the USA
Middletown, DE
07 December 2018